My dearest Birdie

First published in 2007
by Jessica Kingsley Publishers
116 Pentonville Road
London N1 9JB, UK
and
400 Market Street, Suite 400
Philadelphia, PA 19106, USA

www.jkp.com

Library of Congress Cataloging in Publication Data
A CIP catalog record for this book is available from the Library of Congress

British Library Cataloguing in Publication Data
A CIP catalogue record for this book is available from the British Library

ISBN 978 1 84310 635 7

Printed digitally by Lightning Source (UK)

My dearest Birdie
Letters to Australia 1874 to 1886

by Richard and Jessie Gowlland

*Edited by Juliet Phillips
and Richard Joscelyne*

Photographs from the family album

The Story Behind the Letters

The sorting and copying of these letters, written between 1874 and 1885 by Richard and Jessie Gowlland to Richard's sister Celia in Australia, has been more than a labour of family piety. It has been enjoyable and rewarding both to catch an intimate picture of Richard and Jessie, their families and their friends, and to discover the quality of the letters themselves. Richard was an excellent letter writer in that he wrote in elegant, clear and sometimes forceful English. But he was also often bored by the whole business of letter writing (a characteristic of many Civil Servants) so that over the years his letters tend to deteriorate in frequency and in interest, and occasionally in quality. However, even the later ones spring back to life when something touches his imagination or emotions.

Seventy-two letters have been preserved in whole or in part, despite the fact that they have travelled around the world in the century and a quarter since they were written. After Richard's death in 1886, Celia sent them back to England for Jessie to keep. Mildred, Jessie's youngest daughter, was entrusted with them after her mother's death and became in effect the family archivist. Anne-Louise Watts, Mildred's only grandchild, inherited the letters from her and later took them to Canada where she settled with her family. It was there, some years later, that Veronica, Effie's granddaughter, decided to transcribe some of these letters stored in Anne-Louise's basement and to present them to her mother, Rosalind, who as a child had been especially close to Jessie. Soon after they came to Juliet's notice – she had done research on the Whitcombe family but knew little about the Gowllands until she started to read the letters to Birdie. Finally, Anne-Louise brought all the letters back to England and gave them to Juliet who hoped to transcribe them and send them to interested family members. This task, begun with enthusiasm, was to prove daunting and it is thanks to another Richard, great grandson to both Richard and Jessie Gowlland and to Louisa and Henry Joscelyne, that this original plan has been achieved. During several visits to England he helped to organize the chaos of papers, offered endless encouragement – and finally typed out most of the Juliet's transcriptions himself at home in Australia. So in effect the letters have travelled a second circle.

Several of the oldest family members have offered invaluable help by filling in our background knowledge of family friends mentioned in the letters and as to what happened to some of the characters in their old age. The late Langton Gowlland, twin son of little Edward, remembered Jessie taking him and his brother to take tea with Great Aunt Trot, by then widowed and living in London: "She was very dignified, well-turned out and pretty.... tea would be served with great ceremony with a lovely lacy cloth and she gave us a shilling – or it might have been half a crown." Similarly Christopher, Harry Whitcombe's youngest son, remembers being invited as a schoolboy to tea with Willie and Effie Whitcombe, then living in Brighton, and being thrilled by Uncle Willie's stereoscope "which showed startling 3D-type pictures of The Pyramids and things." In Australia our vital link has been Eleanor Barron, daughter of Jack Gowlland's second son, Percy. She has been able to identify several unlabelled photographs in a family album which Juliet discovered on top of an old cupboard after her parents had died. We have used some of these to illustrate the leading characters in "My dearest Birdie".

It is a great pleasure that so many cousins have become involved in the compiling of these letters, a number of whom had never met each other before and are now friends. And now Jessica Kingsley, Jessie's namesake and great granddaughter, has nobly taken on the task of publication. We hope that future generations will use the book as an opportunity to get to know each other – and maybe to follow another trail into our family history.

Most of these letters were written on flimsy paper to ensure the cheapest cost by sea mail and it is their frail state today which has given us the sense of urgency to transcribe and print them. They have been preserved as family treasures through four generations and have been read and re-read. In some cases, the temptation to write over worn phrases or to repair tears with sellotape has made them even more difficult to decipher. Richard Gowlland wrote most of the letters but those few written by Jessie add a good deal to the story. With the exception of one letter written to Alick Oliver to congratulate him on his marriage, they are addressed to Celia, mostly using her nickname "Birdie". We have transcribed all that is legible even when the fragments are incoherent. Richard uses frequent abbreviations and these we have attempted to transcribe consistently (w'd; sh'd; c'd). In the interest of clarity we have occasionally modified the punctuation and introduced some paragraphing, particularly in the early letters which wander on excessively. In some cases we have had to guess at illegible words or add some to preserve the sense – all these have been added in italic script.

We have added an essay on the Gowlland Family and a simple family tree, using the names by which they are known in the letters, of the children and grandchildren of Thomas and Mary Gowlland, Richard's parents, to explain frequent references to family members and to take the story up to Jessie's death in 1935. In addition we have adjoined a number of footnotes to the text , both to elucidate sometimes obscure references to contemporary people and events and to translate occasional passages written in German as well as a number of "old" words which may be strange to us today.

Juliet Phillips
Richard Joscelyne

Jessie Katharine Gowlland

Richard Gowlland

Introduction

In February 1874, John Thomas Ewing (Jack) Gowlland RN, newly promoted to the rank of Commander, and his sister Eliza Celia Gowlland left England to travel across the Continent to Brindisi. From there they sailed to Alexandria, through the newly opened Suez Canal to Aden, Galle and Melbourne before arriving in Sydney on May 18th.

Jack was returning from leave to his post as head of the New South Wales Hydrographical Survey, and to rejoin his wife Genevieve (Jeannie) and his three young children. Celia joined him in order to help with the upbringing of Jack's three children as he evidently had some doubts about his wife's ability in this regard.

Things did not turn out as expected. Jack was carrying out a survey in Sydney harbour; barely three months after his return from leave, when a freak wave overturned his small boat. After assuring himself that his crew had safely swum ashore, he struck out for shore himself, was overcome by cramp, and drowned. He was 36 years old.

The death of her brother must have been as devastating for Celia as it was for Jeannie and her family. But whereas Jeannie was able to rely on the support of her family, Celia found it difficult to get on with her sister in law, and her brother Fred, away in Wagga Wagga, seems to have been rather indifferent to her situation.

Jeannie was the daughter of Percy Lord and grand daughter of Simeon Lord who had been transported to Australia for the theft of some lengths of cloth in Bradford. Simeon became an outstanding merchant and entrepreneur and amassed one of the largest fortunes in the early history of the Australian colonies. Jack had met Percy Lord in an earlier visit to Australia and seems to have formed an attachment to his daughter at that time. In any case they were married soon after his arrival in Sydney in 1865.

After Jack's death Celia may have thought of returning to England as soon as her health had fully benefited from the climate. However, within a year she was married to Alexander Oliver. Alick Oliver had been a close friend of Jack. They had met in perilous circumstances. In 1872 Jack had volunteered to command a relief expedition in the search for the Brigadeen "Maria" which had been chartered by a group of fortune hunters on a search for gold in what is now Papua New Guinea and was wrecked off Bramble Reef in a then remote part of Queensland. Alick Oliver volunteered to join the relief expedition, which found the wreck and rescued 36 pitiful survivors. At the celebratory dinner marking Jack's triumphant return to Sydney, he was presented with some handsome pieces of plate, and a poem "Hail to thee Man of Kent!" was recited to the assembled company by its author Alick Oliver. Alick became one of the most distinguished men of late Victorian and Edwardian Sydney, an eminent lawyer, Parliamentary draftsman and author. He had travelled to England to be educated at Exeter College, Oxford and had been called to the Bar before returning to Australia.

Jack and Celia came from a family of nine children. Their Father, Thomas Sankey Gowlland was a Coastguard whose career took him to Columbkill in Donegal, the Isle of Sheppey, the Scilly Islands, Cornwall and Leigh on Sea in Essex. Mary, their Mother, came from the notable Scottish Irish family of Ewing. Her Mother was a Cathcart and both these names were given to children of the succeeding three generations with obvious pride.

Of the boys, the two eldest, Jack and James, became naval officers. Jack had had a distinguished career, winning a medal for his exploits in the Baltic during the Crimean War. He took part in the Survey of the Western Coast of Canada, helping to define the maritime borders with the United States before being posted to the Colony of New South Wales. Both died young. James was only 17 when he died of yellow fever off Jamaica in 1862.

Richard, the author of the letters, was the third son. He had had from childhood a very close relationship with his sister Celia, whom he called Birdie, and her departure for Australia caused him much grief and anxiety. He had been, according to family legend, the Private Secretary to the Secretary to the Viceroy of India. This may have been at the India Office in Whitehall as there is nothing in the letters that suggests he had been to India. By 1874 he was working at the Office of Public Building and Works. We know very little about his early life. He certainly spent some time studying in France and Germany and wrote very good German. His sister Celia accompanied him on at least some of his journeys to the Continent and shared his knowledge of German. Richard was evidently an outstanding Civil Servant who rose to be deputy head of his department before his early death. The letters paint a vivid picture of his courtship and marriage to Jessica Lake and the birth and childhood of their six children. It was evidently an extremely happy marriage although Richard found it difficult to get on with Jessie's Father and Stepmother in Gravesend.

Frederick William, the fourth son, although originally destined for a naval career, followed his eldest brother to Australia in 1866 at the age of 17. He worked for the Commercial Bank, and was the manager in Wagga Wagga for the whole period of these letters. He married Augusta Mary Wellman in 1874 and had a family of two sons (one of whom died in infancy) and five daughters. The longest surviving of the Gowlland brothers, he was drowned in Botany Bay in 1897.

Annie was the eldest child. She was born in 1832 and died unmarried in 1894. Probably the least gifted of a lively and attractive family, she held various posts as companion and governess and as a lay sister of the Anglican Community of St John the Baptist. There was a long-standing family connection with the Community of St John, which were founded in Ewer near Windsor in 1851 initially to rehabilitate 'fallen women' in a 'House of Mercy'. Annie also spent some considerable periods of time living with Richard and Jessie.

The second daughter, Louisa, married Henry Joscelyne in 1855 when she was barely 20. Henry was at the time studying for his ordination, while acting as private tutor to the Marquesses of Bath. On the urging of the Marquess and his family, Henry went up to Oxford in 1856 soon after the birth of their eldest child Louisa (Lilly). Henry supported his growing family during his studies by acting as Headmaster of the Oxford Middle School and as chaplain of the Oxford Gaol. During the period of the letters he was Curate in Charge of the Parish of Fewcott before being given the living of Ibstone cum Fingest. His delayed preferment was a matter of some considerable unhappiness.

Sarah, the third daughter, always known as Trot, married Philip Whitcombe, a medical practitioner in Gravesend and Medical Adviser to the Port of London. He was some 20 years her senior and the marriage was not a happy one. By 1874 they were living separate lives, although they shared the same house. Family tradition is that they addressed not one word to each other for a period of 40 years. There were four sons of the marriage, Percy, Harry, Willie and Arthur.

Celia was the youngest daughter. She was known affectionately to her brother as Birdie from some childhood game in which Richard had played the part of Wolfie. Of all the sisters, Celia made the 'best' marriage. Although Alick was almost 20 years her senior, and had lost one arm as a boy in a hunting accident, they had nine children together, four boys and five girls and seem to have lived in some style in a large house, 'Shelcote', beside Sydney harbour. Celia, the four sons and three of the five daughters survived Alick's death in 1904. She died in Hornsby, New South Wales, in 1921.

Richard's death from a lung tumour at the age of 40 was devastating for his young family. Apart from the grief on the loss of an exceptional husband and father, Jessie had to bring them up on a small Civil Service pension, and the generosity of family and friends. They remained at the house in Ealing for about ten years before moving to what seems to have been a charming and spacious cottage in Hardwick, where Trot's son Harry was then Vicar; it was from there that Effie and Mildred were married, the former to her cousin Trot's son Willie. Edward, through the generosity of Richard's great friend Rev.Alfred Cooper, studied medicine, became a medical practitioner, served in the RAMC in the Great War with distinction, rising to the rank of Colonel and being awarded a DSO. After the war he became the first Commandant of the Star and Garter Home. He was also the inventor of TCP. His twin sons Geoffrey and Langton became naval officers, serving with distinction in the Second World War. Richard's younger son Geoffrey became a Brigadier in the Royal Engineers was mentioned in despatches during the Great War and served in India. Poor Kitty remained unmarried and died

Celia Oliver née Gowlland

Celia Olivers daughter (?)

Jack Gowlland

Maud

aged 33 of tuberculosis after spending a period of time as a family help in India.

Louisa Joscelyne who lived until 1923 at her daughter Mary's school in Bournemouth, saw her three younger sons become medical practitioners. Her eldest son Harry prospered in Australia, becoming a senior officer in the Federal Meteorological Office. Sadly his two sons were killed in the Great War.

Trot despite her catastrophic illnesses also lived into her eighties and saw her son Harry Whitcombe became Archdeacon and Suffragan Bishop of Colchester.

Eleanor Barron, Jack's grand daughter by his younger son Percy, lives in Bowral in New South Wales and has done much to perpetuate the memory of her grandfather's achievements in Australia. She has kept in touch with her British cousins. She has a large archive of Jack's letters and logs and remembers meetings with Fred's son and daughters.

The families of Jeannie Gowlland and Celia Oliver were not close and beyond the bare bones of the New South Wales Register of Births Marriages and Deaths and the entry for Alexander Oliver in the Australian Biographical Dictionary, sadly we know nothing of the Oliver family.

In her later years Jessie lived with her widowed daughter Effie and her grand children, Marjorie and Mervyn, in Wimbledon. There is a charming photograph of her in 1932 aged 77 attending the Wimbledon wedding of her grand daughter Rosalind to Patrick Joscelyne, the grandson of her sister in law Louisa. In 1935 her great grandchild Anne Joscelyne drew attention to a black mark on her arm, caused by a knife cut while Jessie was chopping up meat. Marjorie thought "Oh, Little Granny is going to die!" And so, after a long life full of vicissitudes, but still with vivid memories of an exceptionally happy marriage and a clutch of bright and successful children, she died of septicaemia on February 25th 1935.

1874

11 Wrotham Road,
Gravesend

1 April 1874

My darling Birdie,

We received all y'r letters from Paris, Macon, Turin, Venice and Brindisi and were delighted to know that your journey so far had been so pleasant and prosperous. I hope the cold you were suffering from at Brindisi soon left you. I concluded you were well at Alexandria or Jack w'd have mentioned you in his telegram from there on 27th. March which I rece'd the same evening. I have been thinking constantly of you, of course, and tracing your course in imagination ever since you left. I read in the Times that the "Hydaspes"* left Suez on the 28th. March, and shall be looking out soon for a telegram from Aden, which sh'd be in Saturday's Times. It is still to me like a dream that you are gone, altho' we have thought about it so long – I longer than you - still it seems to me that you have been flashed away without warning, and indeed the longer warning we might have had the more impossible it w'd be to realise that your departure had really taken place. I wrote to Fred. by the Brindisi mail and enclosed a little note for you. I thought that although it wd. be a short letter you would be glad to see my writing so soon after your arrival.

---

* The Hydaspes (595 tons) had originally been built as a screw driven steamship in 1852 for the mail run from Plymouth to Calcutta. She was converted into a sailing ship in 1868 and used mainly to carry migrants to New Zealand. She very often sailed out of Gravesend. Her long serving and popular captain, Mr Babot, may have been known to Jack. The diaries of a number of migrants have been preserved in libraries and archives in New Zealand and South Australia. She usually seemed to have sailed non-stop to New Zealand from Gravesend. The Suez Canal had been opened five years previously.

I have been going on since yr. departure exactly as you wd. have expected, up and down to Gravesend every day by the express trains and sometimes Trot meets me at the station and we go for a walk together. Sometimes I come straight here, have tea and go for a walk alone, then come back to supper and read and smoke and think about you and Jack ploughing your way across the ocean.

On Saturday I went to see Mrs. Cooper* at Brighton. Saturday was a beautiful day. I reached Brighton at 3 and walked along the parade till dinner time. The place was crowded. I had a swim at Brills – the large bathing-place there - and then had one of their long dinners, talking principally about Cooper; then I walked down to the Aquarium where there was a good crowd and a good Concert; went back to Sussex Sqr. for tea at 10 o'clock, then read out all Cooper's letters to his mother from Cairo. I think she was glad to have me to read than leave them to her their... for Coopers quaint writing is not easily made out; and I half suspect that Mrs. Cooper had skipped some of it. By bedtime the wind had risen, and I heard it howling then and all next day. I was delighted to think that you were far away from the Bay of Biscay. I have never been in such a gale as blew on Sunday. I had to go to St. Pauls by the back way: it was simply impossible for a man and his hat to walk along the front. In the afternoon it was bad and rained a little so I went down to a kind of cave facing the sea, and smoked and watched the sea tearing up the beach in great white breakers. The sea I think never looks so wild when one is out in a ship, as when one looks at it from the shore. I am sure I hope and pray you may not have had any experiences on your way out to make you of a different opinion.

---

*   The widowed mother of Rev Alfred Cooper and HS Cooper. Rev Alfred Cooper was Richard's closest and most generous friend. Although a clergyman he never took a church appointment and spent long periods in Egypt and Palestine.

Cooper's letters from Cairo are very interesting. He gives as good a picture of the place as any I have read; it quite brings it before one. I wonder if you saw him on your way out? But I shall probably hear from him before I hear from you, unless indeed your Suez letter comes here before I hear from him: he has only sent me two letters since he reached Egypt.

We have had all the papers full of the return of the troops from the Ashanti expedition, there have been reviews and dinners and banquets to soldiers and officers and presentations of Victoria Crosses and orders, only two men got Victoria Crosses, Lord Gifford (a mere boy) and a sergeant in the Highland regiment: they both behaved in a very heroic manner. Tell Jack Sir Garnet* especially praised the Marines and Blue Jackets in his speech last night at the Lord Mayor's Banquet. He spoke more highly of the Marines than of any other body under his command.

I enclose your portraits; those that are left that is. I have kept four for myself and have given away all the rest as you directed. Mrs. Butterworth and Louisa Busbridge have not rd. the receipts. Mrs. Butterworth wrote a nice letter and asked me to tell her of yr. arrival when I heard from you.

I heard from Annie today – a doleful letter. She has had a fresh and worse attack of rheumatism and seems to be very desponding as to her future. "What's to become of me?" she says – as if she had not got a friend or relation in this world. You must get Fred and Jack not to forget to help me keep the poor old girl going. Of course I know how willing they are to do it if they only remember it.

Old Whitcombe has just declined point blank to give Trot any clothes, so I have written to him on the subject, and if he does not supply her in a week, I am going to give her the money

---

*   Sir Garnet Wolseley. In fact four Victoria Crosses were awarded in the 1873/74 Ashanti Campaign.

Jessie K Gowlland, with eldest son
Edward

Jessie K Gowlland

Jack John Gowlland (?)

Richard Gowlland (?)

she wants and to sue him in the Crown Court for the amount: this will be very unpleasant but it is the only thing to do. I am glad that Jack was spared that worry while he was in England.

I shall close for tonight and write a little more in London before posting this.

                                        11 Wrotham Road,
                                        Gravesend

                                        8th May 1874

Darling Birdie,

We have been rejoiced, Trot and I, to read in the papers that the March mail arrived in Melbourne on the 4th. This is two days earlier than the time stated on the list of arrivals you left with us. I hope it means that you have had an extraordinarily prosperous voyage. We had seen nothing of yr. ship since you left Aden. Your arrival at Galle was not telegraphed. We are looking now, anxiously for your letter from there. You took 30 days to get there if you had gone via Southampton so that about the 12th. I shall expect to get a letter. I am looking forward to it immensely, indeed, more than anything else on my horizon at present.

I had a letter from Fred today. I am sorry to hear that he is going to be away from Sydney for a long time at so remote a place as Wagga Wagga. Odd how he'd go to the place of all others that is known better than any other place in Australia to all English speaking people - there must be millions of Englishmen who have never heard of Sydney or Melbourne who could tell you all about Wagga-Wagga from its connection to the Tichborne case. I see in the paper today that there has been a petition to Govt. to release that scoundrel Orton.* It is inconceivable that there should be so many fools in the world.

I have just been talking for two hours with Trot. I haven't seen her since we were at the Fletchers together. She came back yesterday - she and Arthur looking better for being away. The Fletchers have been very kind and she is under orders to pay them a long visit with all the Boys in July. The boys will not object. They will have cricket and birds nests to their heart's desire.

Yesterday evening I went to S: Pauls. The Gregorian Choral Union had an innings. Coates and I and his choir went – we were at the Cathedral doors at ¼ to six. Doors opened at half past six; immense rush of crowd through the doors – and rush down the nave to reach the seats under the dome: poor Coates' crutches slipped on the pavement and over he went on his face cutting his knee. We picked him up and we got good seats – too near in fact and waited patiently till eight when the service began. There were then twelve thousand people in the Cathedral; a thousand men and boys in the Choir in surplices: it was a wonderful sight: there were silver trumpets and euphoniums to keep them together. They sang 2 processionals – one "Oh sons and daughters of the King". It sounded perfect. The Service was closed by the Te Deum and was not over till half past ten. The recessional was "Jesu the very thought was sweet".

I walked to the temple to see H.S. Cooper after the service: he was not at home fortunately; his mother is always asking me to go to see him; I am going down to see her on Sunday week.

I walked on from there to Upper Glo'ster Place where I slept: it seemed very desolate. I dislike sleeping elsewhere I don't live

---

* Orton, a bankrupt butcher from Wagga Wagga, claimed to be the long-lost heir to the Tichborne Baronetcy and fortune. The subsequent court case was the longest, most expensive and most sensational in British legal history. Orton was subsequently sentenced to 14 years hard labour for perjury.

– which I take to be an early sign of old bachelor-hood !!! I expect I shall be an old bachelor after all; it all seems impossible that I shall ever meet a girl whose qualities hit off my wishes or rather requirements – one wants such opposite things: Youth and wisdom, money and modesty, taste without vanity, etc. etc. etc. I am beginning to give it up. I have been talking a long time with Trot on the subject this evening and I begin to think it is out of the question. But now I will comfort myself with a pipe and leave all these matters to right themselves.

11th.May. I have just read you long letter from Ceylon. I was delighted to hear that you have been enjoying the voyage and that you had not met with rough weather. The verses you sent apropos of the voyage are well written – the man evidently has a gift in that direction. He's more interesting than one of the Passengers in Fred's ship who wrote beautiful verses. Fred sent me some of them and they were Hood's composition. We never saw yr. arrival in Sydney advertised but as of course you reached Melbourne on the 4th, you were there long ago.

I had a letter from Cooper today – he is at Alexandria on his way back. I think he must be coming back via Greece as he is going to Smyrna.

The Emperor of Russia lands here on Wednesday. We have a fleet of Ironclads again here and at Thames Haven. I wish Jack were here to take us off to see some of them.

We had Athletic Sports here on Saturday – it rained the whole time. I caught a frightful cold, which makes me "redface and brooms".

A new Secretary was appointed to our office today – Mr. Mitford*, quite young, 35. The Asst. Sec. Mr. Callander is

* Algernon Freeman Mitford, later Lord Redesdale, was appointed by Disraeli as Permanent Secretary of the Department of Public Building and Works after returning from Japan where he had been Secretary at the British

therefore passed over. You may think, therefore, whether he is pleased. I suppose the clerks of the Treasury could not afford but to give away so good and rare a prize as £1200 a year to one of their friends.

20 May. I have not written anything to you for 9 days I see. I don't know why except, perhaps, that I have had a bad cold and stiff neck and have felt idle. Gravesend has been in a state of excitement all through the week. The Czar of Russia* was to land here on Wednesday but his ship ran ashore at Flushing so he landed at Dover instead. He has promised to embark from here for Russia tomorrow. There have been great doings in London: procession to the city, fetes at Crystal Palace, Expedition to Woolwich, reviews and so on. A good many people have been nervous lest some of the Polish Refugees shd. take it into their heads to have a shot at the Czar. He is always accompanied by an immense body of Police and they say that Gravesend is filled with Detectives to look after suspicious characters. The officers of the English ship here, the Triumph, gave a dance on board their ship last night. I did not go but most of the girls who dance rec'd invitations. The town gave the officers a dance at the Institution the day the Czar was to have landed. I dined with the Framshaws that night and went to the dance afterwards. We danced to near 3 from 9. All the usual people were there. There were a number of Russian officers who danced queerly – danced across the room like rockets. The Polka is their favourite dance. They are little men and do not look very refined. They behave however very well. Their uniforms are just like ours except they have no fringe to their epaulettes.

Legation in Yokohama. He wrote a notable book on Meiji Japan. He was the grandfather of the Mitford sisters.

*   Tsar Alexander II. He was the last Russian Head of State to make a State Visit to England before Vladimir Putin in 2003.

I saw the Czar this morning and yesterday – a fine looking man; is always wrapped up in a great heavy cloak. The Princess of Wales is always the most popular person in the Royal procession. She always looks so cheerful and appears to be enjoying herself and then she is so pretty and always dresses with such good taste. The ladies here now wear tight-fitting bonnets, which swallow up all their hair behind but I am told the very newest thing in bonnets is a bonnet without any crown at all but merely a wreath covering the same ground which a Roman laurel wreath would.

I rec'd Jack's telegram yesterday at 2 o'clock (19 May) despatched from Sydney on the 18th at 6 p.m. This is at any rate an assurance that you are both safely arrived at Sydney.

28 May 74. I went to Fewcott on Saturday; found the baby ill. Dr. came on Sunday and after examining baby examined all the other children and sent five of them to bed and enquired after the drains and the water. He came again on Monday and after being a great deal pressed said he thought they had diphtheria. After looking at them however carefully he said he did not think it was so serious but still thought it wise for me to depart wh. I did the same evening instead of remaining till Wednesday morning as I had originally intended. I hear from Trot today that Lilly writes that they are all ill except Louisa…

… brother-in-law & sister & children who had just arrived from India. No bed to be had in the house, the first floor being let to two Turks. I turned out to try and find a bed – wandered about for about half an hour, found nothing and came back purposely to sleep on a sofa – but the Dr. wdn't hear of this and insisted on giving up his bed; he being a shorter man did better on sofa than I sh'd. I went to ?Medley to spend the day. It was very beautiful weather had an early dinner and…

Fragment of a letter written
in June 1874

Have I told you that the long talked of Treasury Committee is coming at last? They are going to sit upon us next week. It is expected that all the "old screws" will be weeded out, and that the rest of us – for you see I assume I am not considered a "screw" - will get better pay. I haven't much faith in the present Government treating us liberally. We have found their performances lag far behind their promise – and they have had so many hangers on to provide with good places that they have been unable to venture to further swell the Estimates by satisfying the claims of the permanent staff of the Civil Service.

Beach Road, Deal
9 July 1874

My dearest Birdie,

You will have received my last two letters in which I told you in German how I thought at last I remarked a thawing on the part of Jessie Lake. I remember that when you were in England I had almost given up thinking it possible that she would ever care for me, and I really avoided going to the house because I did not want to get in love with a girl who did not love me. Still she continued very continually in my remembrance by a sort of instinct I suppose, and when a month or two ago I observed the thawing referred to I made the most of the few opportunities I had of seeing her. Well the long and the short of it is that the slow growth of six months grew more rapidly in the last month of the six. As I told you in my last letter, I came down to Deal to settle the question one way or another. I cannot tell you how great an anxiety it has been to me for a long time past. I have not talked about it in my letters because I was so very doubtful whether Jessie thought at all of me. You will wonder that I have not said more about it, but the fact is one doesn't talk much of a subject about which one is deeply in earnest.

I came then down to Deal last Wednesday week – of course I had great opportunities of seeing Jessie. I could not make out a bit whether she cared for me, she is so extremely shy and reserved. I could stand the suspense no longer and proposed to her on Friday evening. Well then I found out she had loved me all along and that all the coldness and reserve was assumed towards me that, I suppose, I might not suspect the truth. I can't tell you, my darling, how extremely extravagantly happy I am about it. Now that all the past is opened up and I know Jessie much better, I feel that if I had not been accepted by her I should not have married anyone. I certainly could not love another girl as I love her – and when I tell you I love her with all my heart you will know from your knowledge of me that this love includes the highest respect and admiration.

I am sorry you did not know more of her before you left. She is the dearest sweetest best little girl in all the world. It is five days since we are engaged and my only feeling is that I am not half good enough for her. I cannot conceive that I shall in the longest life ever have any other regret about the matter except that; I never before conceived it possible that I should fall so deeply in love with anyone. It seems to me to be an opening up of quite a new world of hopes and feelings. I never before knew the happy appearance and the joyfulness which the world can present. One seems to love everyone more and I know certainly my darling I love you more and I know that you will sympathise with me in these new relations more heartily than anyone else can because of the great love we have always had for one another. You may rely upon it, my darling, that I can have made no mistake in my choice.

Genevieve Lord M John Ewing
Gowlland, the belle of Sydney

Jack John Ewing Gowlland

Maude Gowlland, daughter of Jack
and Genevieve

Jessie sends you her love and all manner of kind things. Our engagement has been announced to her aunts, who all seem extremely fond of her, and they and the rest of her family congratulate her upon her choice. Those who have seen me think that I shall make a good husband. Of course not a word has been said about when the climax will be, but I suppose, this time next year at the earliest. I hope by then I shall be promoted – there appears to be every prospect of it. We have a Treasury Commission sitting at our office at the present moment and everyone thinks I shall get promoted through it. Mr. Lake was extremely kind about it. He seemed to expect it when I told him.

As you can imagine it has been a very happy holiday for me. Deal is otherwise rather a dull place but in these circumstances, of course, things have worn the most joyful aspect. The Lakes unfortunately go away today. I am going to see them as far as Canterbury. I remain here with Trot until Monday when, we return to Gravesend. Our engagement is to be kept quiet for a fortnight in order that all the rest of the family may know before the public talk about it. They are a very sensitive family and have to be treated with great attention. Jessie is the favourite of certain old aunts from whom she has reasonable prospects and so Mrs Lake is very anxious that they should be pleased about this and so far they appear to be very pleased.

We saw Annie the other day at Gravesend. She came down for the day. She is so much improved by being with the Sisters: her face looks different and she seems to be perfectly contented.

Jessie you may remember is just 18 – 19 next February, so there are just ten years between us but she has the wisdom of a much greater age.

Cooper came over to see us last night. Of course he was very anxious to see Jessie. He is very pleased with her, thinks her extremely pretty. She has certainly the sweetest smile conceivable.

...I am writing at the Lakes and Jessie is sitting opposite nursing her little sister, and her pretty eyes beam when I look up, so if this letter is incoherent, as I know it must be, it is her fault and not mine, for how can a man remain reasonable with such suns shining on him! Jessie sends her love to Jack, whom she remembers perfectly. She says she saw a good deal of him and talked a good deal to him. I did not know this. Trot will tell me all the news and post this for me. Will you tell Jack all about this? I have no time to write him a special letter.

...Goodbye my own dearest sister and believe me now and always your most affectionate brother R.S.G.

Fragment written in July or
August 1874

...Perhaps I ought not to speak of immense trouble though, but you understand a thing which calls for one's attention in the City when one ought to be in Whitehall is irritating.

Jessie sends you her love and her Photograph – the latter is too old for her everyone says, and I don't think it is nearly pretty enough for her – of course her smile is lost and she has the most sweet smile I have ever seen on anyone's face – it lights up her face in a remarkable manner – then she has shut her mouth in the Photograph which is contrary to nature – her mouth is always enough open to show the tips of two very white teeth – all this you will perhaps think unnecessary information since you yourself have seen her; then, you see, you haven't looked at her as much as I have lately. She has not yet got at all used to my looking at her and is quite confused if I stare straight into her eyes for two seconds!! She is indeed in every way very simple and childlike and yet in other things very wise and self possessed and "grown up". She doesn't play much but has learnt all the accompaniments to my songs and is under the fond delusion that I sing like Apollo. She sings a little but is much to shy to sing before me more than once in a new moon. I am over at the Lakes certainly 6 evenings out of seven. I always dine and have supper there on Sunday. The other evenings we generally get long talks together in the drawing room while the rest of the family is in the dining room. We keep dreadfully late hours I am afraid. It is difficult to get away early! Jessie is always at the window to wave adieu to me as I go to get the train. She looks so beautiful and bright and radiant that it is like a new and better sunshine just to see her for that moment in passing. She has just given me a locket to contain her portrait and on Saturday wk. last we came up to town together to get another photograph taken small enough to go into the locket. If it is a good one I will send a copy to you; but we haven't had the proof yet.

Last Saturday Trot and her two boys and Jessie Mary and two of their little sisters Grant and myself took a wagonette and drove to the hills which you see from Malling. We arrived there about 4 made tea on the hills and had a little pic-nic; and a nice walk afterwards. We came back about 9 o'clock. Such a moon and such a night.

I haven't been away on my leave yet and you can imagine don't want much to go – but I think I shall go to Brighton to spend the 3 weeks I have left; during that time Jessie will I expect pay some visits to her Aunts. It is a rather a wild proceeding I still think our being engaged for I see no prospect at present of our being married. There is no sign of promotion in my office. We have a new Secretary – a very nice man called Mitford late Secretary to the Legation at Yokohama. Goodbye my darling – I hope you find the new climate agrees with you and that you have no worries of any kind. Believe me always your affectionate brother R.S.Gowlland.

11 Wrotham Rd,
Gravesend

20/Oct. 74

My Darling Birdie,

You will be thinking of us all here and especially at this time when you know we shall first hear the awful news of our dear Brother's death. How strange it seems that we have been going on just the same for the last two months while he was lost to us. But I am glad you did not send a telegram for I should have hoped against hope – I am afraid we all should – and disbelieved it. Even now everyone who comes to sympathize with me is sure to ask whether it is quite certain to be true – a violent death always suggests so certainly the prospect of escape. Dear Jack I am sure often thought that such would or might be his end. He has so often talked to me about the perils he had passed through on the sea and often wound up with the words that he could see his way to leave a service which he had no hesitation in calling especially dangerous.

I have just received letters from Fewcott where Trot and Annie are with Louisa. You will no doubt hear of them – they are all, as you w'd expect to hear, dreadfully distressed. As for me I never felt so much anything in my life - I had learnt to love Jack very dearly. His frank genial honest nature was something so unusually pleasant and amiable that it was impossible not to feel more and more drawn to him; and he was so bright and alive and energetic that one felt more and more proud of him as one knew him better. His loss will be a perpetual regret to all of us.

I have written a long letter to Fred, which you must read and I have also written to Jeannie. Poor thing she and the boys and Maudie are the greatest sufferers by this calamity – they have lost everything – one trembles to think what a loss it is to the boys. To lose a father is bad enough but one who was so devoted to them – whose every effort was directed to their benefit – is a great loss indeed.

About yourself, my darling, it is so very very sad for you – it is entirely unlooked for since it has swept away the…

> Fragments of letter written
> in late november or early
> december 1874

… I was rather surprised not to hear from you by this mail. Fred wrote on the 23rd.nearly 10 days after the accident so that I shd. have thought you might have had time to write. I have not recd. the newspaper Fred speaks of sending, but a newspaper wh. was sent to me in connection with the coal business contained an account of the accident and dear Jack's funeral.

My dear little Jessie was very sorry to hear the bad news. She had seen Jack, you know, and liked him very much; indeed all the Lakes did as indeed who is there who ever saw him who did not. She at once put on mourning for him and no one could sympathize more genuinely with me in this great sorrow than she has done. Trot being away from Gravesend, I had no one else I could talk to about the dear fellow. I am sure, my darling, you will love dear Jessie. I love her more and more every day – indeed I suppose people would call my love for her a wild infatuation. I am sure I could not love anyone I am engaged to more, and the joy I experience in seeing her every day is not a whit the less because it comes so often. I cannot tell you what a sweet bright loving child she is – it seems too good to be true that she will, if we live, some day be my wife. She is so pretty too when she smiles. I never thought I could be so in love with anyone but I suppose it is what happens to most people. I don't think tho' most people adore their wives as I do now adore Jessie.

I don't know when we shall be married. I haven't any chance of furnishing a house for at least two years to come and then it will only be the result of a long period of pinching and scraping. I can't bear the thought it will be put off so long a time, but I really don't see how it can be done sooner unless the coal mine is sold and something is given to me for getting it sold – but I can't rely on that even now, because I had no arrangement with Jack and all the Commission £5000 would go to his Estate altho' it is I who have done all the work, but it isn't sold yet and perhaps may never be.

...(Coal) Mine. Mr. Farmer has written to say he has withdrawn it from his hands. He places the disposal of it in mine till the 31st Inst. when unless I can show him good prospect of selling it he will withdraw it from the London Market. I have placed it in John Lake's hands. He promises to make every effort to sell it. I sincerely hope he may succeed. I am so anxious that dear old Jack's debts sh'd be paid. Give my best love to Jeannie and tell her I will do all I possibly can for her in this matter.

Mr. Oliver's notice is well written...I suppose he...

... then so as to change the appearance. I can't bear to think of all the misery he underwent here poor fellow – I had to get up in the night sometimes to light the fire and boil water for soda bandages to put on his knees and feet – he suffered so; and yet he was never cross – no one could be more patient than he was. He was indeed a fine fellow.

You mention having met Mr. Dawson again. I think the less you and Jeannie see of that sort of person the better; the man with such manners and...w'd not be tolerated in English society and people upon North Shore must indeed be at a great loss for a lion or a hero to be excited over such a person. I sh'd say that he must have got up in manners from the niggers of Central Africa only that he never went there. I beg you not to tolerate a person who has so little respect for the amenities of society.

It is a great trial for me to leave…worst of it I suppose. You will no doubt hear from her this mail!

There could be no sweeter or more amicable girl, She is so kind and loving to everyone. I should like you to see her stop in the street and commiserate with a dirty little child crying. – the child feels happy at once. She is very fond of talking to the little ragamuffins when they are in distress and arranging their quarrels. She is a great ally of the crossing sweepers and they listen with awe to her little hints…and are rather happier to serve… perform very well however. She is wonderfully helpful and kind and everyone indeed, has been enthusiastic and kind for the last month about teaching the cook who can't read or write. The cook has lessons from 8 to 9 every evening! It is most happy and thankworthy, is it not? that I should be engaged to one who has a character beyond all praise and beyond what one could have imagined in its extraordinary kindness lovableness and unselfishness to say nothing of her beautiful beaming face and how she w'd shout with derision if she knew what I have written about her, for she is as unconscious as a baby of all this and simply laughs in my face if I ever venture to intimate that she is better or more beautiful than other people.

We had a sad Sunday evening – my last in Gravesend. She was in tears the whole time. I am to go there for the Xmas holidays – we have holidays from Thursday to Tuesday during which…

Fragment written between 20th October and 4th November 1874

I was rather surprised not to hear from you by this mail. Fred wrote on the 23rd nearly 10 days after the accident so I sh'd

Augusta (?)   Fred

have thought you might have had time to write. I have not rec'd the newspaper Fred speaks of sending, but a newspaper wh. was sent to me in connection with the coal business contained an account of the accident and dear Jack's funeral.

My dear little Jessie was very sorry to hear the bad news. She had seen Jack, you know, and liked him very much; indeed all the Lakes did as indeed who is there who ever saw him who did not. She at once put on mourning for him and no one could sympathise more genuinely with me in this great sorrow than she has done. Trot being away from Gravesend, I had no one else I could talk to about the dear fellow.

I am sure, my darling, you will love my dear Jessie. I love her more and more every day – indeed I suppose people would call my love for her a wild infatuation. I am sure I could not love anyone I am engaged to more, and the joy I experience in seeing her every day is not a whit the less because it comes so often. I cannot tell you what a sweet bright loving child she is – it seems too good to be true that she will, if we live, some day be my wife. She is so pretty too when she smiles. I never thought I could be so in love with anyone but I suppose it is what happens to most people. I don't think tho' most people adore their wives as I do now adore Jessie.

I don't know when we shall be married. I haven't any chance of furnishing a house for at least two years to come and then it will only be the result of a long period of pinching and scraping. I can't bear to think it will be put off so long a time, but I really don't see how it can be done sooner unless the coal mine is sold and something is given to me for getting it sold – but I can't rely much on that even now, because I had no arrangement with Jack and all the Commission £5000 would go to his Estate altho' it is I who have done all the work – but it isn't sold yet and perhaps may never be.

11 Wrotham Road,
Gravesend

4 Nov. 74

My darling Birdie,

Your letters have come at last. They should have come via Brindisi but by some bad arrangement did not come until the Southampton mail with the letters you sent to Trot and Louisa.

I am so grieved for you, my dearest; you must I am afraid have felt terribly lonely during the time which has passed since August. And you do indeed well say that nothing but a firm faith could have supported you in such desolation. Es tut mir sehr leid zu wissen, dass Fritz ein so kalter Mensch ist, aber es ist gerade was ich von dem lieben Jack von ihm gehort habe, er sagte, er ware nie mit ihm halb so bruderlich und offen wie man habe erewarten konnen. Es ist seine Natur, so zuruckhaltend zu sein. Ja es wird mich freuen sehr, wenn du auf Australien den Rucken gegeben hast. Wie werden wir uns freuen, Dich wieder zu sehen.[*]

I am so glad to hear that Mr. and Mrs. Lord are so kind to you. So Jeannie is not going to stay with them as we all expected she would, but is still to have her own little house. I w'd have thought that they w'd have preferred to have them all to themselves. I hope poor girl she will by this time have become a little bit more submissive under the frightfully heavy sorrow she has to bear. It is a merciful thing, dearest, that you are with her and can turn her mind into the only channel where she can receive comfort. I am afraid that if you had not been there, there

---

*   I am sorry to learn that Fritz is such a cold person but it is exactly what I heard about him from dear Jack – he said he had never been as half as brotherly and open with him as one would have expected. It is his nature to be so reserved. Yes, I will be very happy when you have turned your back on Australia. How happy we shall be to see you again.

w'd have been no one who would have pointed out to her how the blow sh'd be received.

5 Nov. I went to see Hawkin yesterday at Redhill. He has taken a large furnished house there and seems as happy as possible. His wife was once engaged to marry Jack. I dare say you have heard. She seemed genuinely sorry to hear his sad news. She is not at all a brilliant woman, but is very quiet and ladylike – has a certain repose and dignity in her manner wh. I sh'd not have expected to come from Vancouver but she has been a good deal in England since then. They entertained me sumptuously and I stayed there all night.

Hawkin was very fond of Jack evidently – he had the highest opinion of him. But he said he thought from his looks when he was in England that he would not have a long life.

Old Mr.Mowlam came to my office to see me today and remained here half an hour. I think he is the dearest old man I ever met – so thoroughly good hearted. I am afraid Jack must have borrowed more money from him than he is likely to repay – but he (Mowlam) never once referred to that. He is going back to Australia on Monday and will arrive about the same time as this letter. His address is Union Club Sydney. He is very bent upon taking up the facts for a biography of Jack and was discomforted when I told him that Oliver had taken the matter up. I could not get facts from either Hawkin or Jackson wh. wd. be of service. I am afraid I shall not see Mowlam again.

I have been to St. James's to church this evening and then afterwards from 9 to 11 I have been at the Lakes.

I have been in dreadfully bad spirits for the last few days – I can't think why. It is very unpleasant and unlike me – I wonder what Jessie thinks of it! I often wonder too if is possible for a girl to alter her opinion about a man and be sorry she ever saw him – but I suppose if she did that w'd indicate an absence of real affection and the sooner that was demonstrated and the bubble burst the better for everyone. Now I must go to bed.

Sat.7 Nov. Trot came back to Gravesend yesterday and I spent the evening with her. She is still very far from well she says, altho' one doesn't notice that she is different from her usual self – Fewcott seems to be a very unhealthy place. Trot had (and also her children) the same sort of bad throat which all the Joscelynes had in the spring when I was there. Trot says Louisa seems in a bad state of health. She suffers from palpitation almost every evening. Trot has not at all become used to dear old Jack's death. She will continue depressed about it in a state of mind I don't sympathise with…a better thing for him and what he himself would have wished if he must meet an early death. He has often spoken to me of the glorious death of a soldier in the field of battle with envy – and that was just what he had only instead of being engaged in fighting fellow creatures, he was for their good braving danger which was far nobler.

His old friend, Jackson, came to see me yesterday and we had a long talk about him. Jackson said Jack had a firm impression always that he w'd some day by some lucky chance become enormously rich. It was an odd impression to have and certainly he never had much to support such an one.

Trot had no difficulty about the mourning – Whitcombe sent it to her at Fewcott at once. He appeared to take some interest in the matter for he opened and read the paper which you sent.

Did I tell you that Harry wrote Trot a charming letter when he heard our bad news. After speaking of his sorrow he said ('curiously enough' crossed out) "it is very extraordinary that one of the psalms which I heard in going into Chapel directly after (CIII) reminded me very much of someone he will meet in heaven." I dare say you remember how Mammie liked to have that psalm read to her. Harry remembered that Trot had told him so. I thought he had said it so well that I have copied his own words out of his letter which I have given. It appears he is making wonderful progress at school, beating every one at Euclid and Arithmetic.

I have just come back from a walk with Grant – the Parson who lives here. He is a capital fellow and I should be sorry to go away from here on his account even if Jessie were not in the question. But I must go and live in town if I ever dream of being married. It is my only chance of saving a little money. I can live much more cheaply in Up.Gl. Pl. (Upper Gloucester Place) than down here so when my season ticket expires wh. it will do on 13th Dec. I shall go back to town. I shall try and see Jessie every Sunday, although I always tell her I shall only come down once a month.

10 Nov. 74. Yesterday the town was filled with commotion. The new mayor had to be elected. The late mayor, Jessie's uncle Wm. Lake, was re-elected by acclamation. In the evening the town was crowded and an immense number of sqibs were let off. Jessie and I viewed the crowd from the Bank, the manager of wh. is a friend of ours. I talked to the Manager about Fred and he shewed me Fred's name in the Bank Directory when he was manager at Burrangong. The 1874 Directory does not contain Wagga Wagga as a branch of the Commercial Bank.

By the way, will you tell Fred his marriage I put into the Times, the Standard, the Daily News and the Pall Mall Gazette, so I should think all the Wellmans in England must have seen it. I have kept the pieces which contain it and will send it to him.

I go to see Trot every day. She does not appear to be nearly as well as one w'd like to see her, complains much of lassitude and can't sleep at night. She is a wonderfully sensitive nature – any sorrow or anxiety seems to get such hold on her. This is not at all the case with me, altho' I am very subject to fits of depression about nothing at all! I am sure I ought to be secure against that kind of thing now, and it is very wrong of me to be otherwise for I have cause to be thankful for every thing. No one could, I think, be more critical of his future wife and the more I get to know of Jessie the more certain I become that she is more than all I could wish her to be. I am so happy to think that there is nothing that I w'd like to see altered in her. I am sure that she is the soul of truth and honesty and genuineness; and then she is so penetrated with a sense of the necessity of holiness in everyone's life. She is in every way so good that I can hardly believe that I am not dreaming sometimes when I think that she will some day be my wife.

This evening (12th. Nov.) we have been spending the evening at Trot's – Annie was there. She has come down to spend a few days with Trot. Trot is better – she is taking a tonic and that is setting her up. She will be glad of Annie's society. As I said before, she dwells too much on the horror of dear Jack's death – a morbid view which it appears to take a long time to efface.

Annie seemed quite well and is happy as usual at Pimlico* – has quite lost her rheumatism, I am happy to say. We were very cheerful. All the girls are very fond of Jessie – Louisa is wonderfully smitten with her. I don't indeed know any girl who is so universally beloved but none of them know as well as I do what a darling she is.

Annie was going to post a long letter to you by this mail and one from Sister but I told her that it w'd go probably quite as soon via San Fransisco which leaves only 4 days later – indeed no doubt you will have her letter sent that way before this reaches you – I write by the first on the chance that it may come a little sooner and that at any rate the letters will not all come in a

---

*   a refuge of the Community of St John the Baptist.

heap. It is better for you and more cheering that they sh'd be distributed.

I think and feel so much for you my dearest – it seems quite unfeeling on my part to say so much of myself and to say so little about what I think of so much – you and your plans and what you may be doing – but I could only repeat what I have said already. I am so longing for your letters to hear how you go on. I hope we shall hear by every mail. For my own sake, for the comfort and satisfaction and happiness you'd be to me I (? wish) you were near me and no longer feeling lonely. I wish you were coming back at once, that you were here now. But for your own future comfort when you do return, I hope you will be able to put up with Australia until that climate has had a good chance of doing all it can for yr. health. It has done so much for other people, so entirely altering and reinvigorating their constitution that I am anxious that neither our impatience to have you once more among us, nor your own to come back sh'd be allowed to interfere with this grand opportunity of setting you up which will not offer itself again.

Goodbye my darling. I am sure you will keep a good heart and believe always that you are continually in our hearts and minds. Jessie means to write via San Francisco. Meanwhile she sends her best love and her thanks for your kind messages. I am sure you will be happier when you come back than you would have ever been before when you find what a dear little sister you will know in Jessie. Maude sends her love too.

Ever your very loving brother R.S.Gowlland. My best love to Fred Gussie and Jeannie.

Henry Whitcombe (Harry became a Bishop)

Jack (Jack and Percy brothers)

Percival Whitcombe

Percy, Eleanore's father

11 Wrotham Road,
Gravesend

18 Nov.74

My dearest Birdie,

Of course the day after I posted my and Jessie's letter to you,
your own letter of the 24th.of Sept. arrived so that you will not
get the receipt acknowledged till much later than you might
have expected. Thank you much for it. My last two letters I have
addressed to St Leonards but those I wrote before that I sent to
Wagga Wagga so no doubt you will be surprized at not hearing
immediately after the mail comes. I quite expected that you
would go up to stay with Fred after being a week or so at Sydney.
I am glad, however, that you are staying at Sydney. It is much
better for you in every way than being at Wagga because, of
course, you could be more useful to Jeannie than you could be to
Gussie; and I suppose there are likely to be more quiet people at
Sydney who knew dear old Jack and would be friendly to his
sister.

I am so sorry to hear that you have a touch of rheumatism.
But surely the hot weather at Sydney will soon drive it away. It is
very odd indeed that you should have it. But you know that I
had an attack when I was 16. I am sorry to hear that you shd. not
feel strong but I am not at all surprised at it; there is nothing
more wearing than grief and anxiety, and you have had a great
deal of that lately. But pray do not let yourself feel down. You
must, if you don't do so, take some iron. I doubt (?whether you
will ever be well enough) entirely to leave it off. But pray if you
ever feel yourself drifting into that lassitude, don't lose a day in
getting your iron prescription made up. I trust really, dearest,
that you will make a point of attending to this wish of mine
without a day's delay. As for your rheumatism, I trust it may be
like Annie's - a mere passing attack. I cannot think it can become

chronic with a girl as young as you are. But pray get what advice you can about it in Sydney.

You refer in yr. letter I see to the fact that Jack's friends noticed frequently since his return to Sydney that he was very absent and absorbed, and they think it might be the beginning of an illness. I do not think this at all. I am sure he was anxious about the repaying of the large sums of money he had borrowed. I have often noticed that he was the same here when he was anxious about anything. I am sure that all the concern he must have felt at all his Coal mining schemes failing was enough to account for his being unusually absent in conversation. Then Fred says in his letter to me that the Doctors seemed to think that his constitution was worn out and that in the ordinary course of things he w'd not have probably lived long. That was not at all the opinion of the Doctors in London – on the contrary they thought his a wonderful constitution, which could stand the violent remedies he took for his foot without any serious results to his general health. I mention this because I don't think an erroneous notion on this subject shd. be handed down to his children. The Doctors here all thought he had seen the worst of his gout.

I can't tell you how much I think of the poor fellow. The first thing when I wake as a rule I find the whole awful scene flash across my mind – the last thing before I go to sleep it is the same and all day long I think of it – much more indeed than I did at first. I would not have believed that his loss w'd have made the world appear so wanting in something. I had so little to do with him when he was away – but now I find that I did unconsciously derive much solid comfort and satisfaction from the knowledge that there was somewhere in the world a kind manly heart and a strong hand which would be always ready to feel for or help me. I have always, I found, been thinking of Jack's house as a second home of mine. I did not know that I ever thought of his

surroundings in that way until he was gone – and there is no one
who can ever occupy in my mind and heart the particular place
which he did. I don't know quite how to express what I mean
but there is a certain lightness and warmth gone out of my
horizon with him and also a certain sense of security which
quite astonish me. No loss that I have ever had has left behind in
my mind such a feeling of dreariness and desolation. We do not
at all know how we depend on those nearest and dearest to us
for happiness. I think I least of all have appreciated this. Really, if
I had not been engaged to Jessie and had that great comfort – her
love – to think about, I don't know what I should have done.

Looking at your letter I find that you reply on the 25th of
Sept. to my letter of the 7th of Aug. and I get the reply on
the18th of Nov. That is wonderfully quick just 14 weeks and 5
days to write and get a reply. I have not heard from Fred since
25th. August. You don't say how long he remained at Sydney
and how he seemed. As he doesn't write to me much you must
let me know how he gets on.

Es ist nicht sondebar, dass du in diese Frau nicht verliebt bist;
sie muss, also die Frauen dort mussen so ganz anders seine von
den Frauen, welche Du zu sehr gewohnt bist. Du musst es dich
nicht kummern lassen, dass Du nicht viel Liebe von diesen
Leuten bekommst. Du musst immer eher denken an die grosse
grosse Liebe, die dich von mir, von den Schwestern, von meinem
lieben kleinen Madchen, ihre Freundinnen hier erwartet -
Gewiss gibt es wenige Madchen, die so viele Liebe haben wie
du. Dieses Bewusstsein sollte dich glucklich machen, obgleich
du so fern von den Liebenden bist. Du musst fortwahrend an
unsere Liebe denken.[*]

***

[*] I do not find it strange that you have not fallen in love with this woman; she
must – the women there must – be quite different from the women to whom
you are so very much accustomed. Don't let it bother you that you are not
receiving much love from these people. You must always think instead of the

I hope very much the Committee who are arranging a monument to be placed over dear Jack's grave will have some Christian emblem on it. I incline much more to the simple white marble cross than the grand expensive tombstone. I hope they won't put up a broken column or inverted torch or urn or any other heathen device. When whatever is decided upon is put up will you try to get a photograph taken; I mean not merely of the stone but of the locality in which it is – the church landscape if possible so that we may always be able to think of where he sleeps. Could you indeed not try to make a painting of it for me.

23 Nov 74. On Saturday Jessie and I went to dine at Six Dawley Road. She looked so pretty dressed up in plain white muslin for the evening! We quite expected the Lakes w'd have been alone or we sh'd not have gone. But Mary and Harry Woodford were there. Harry Woodford amused us. He talks and thinks of nothing but his dogs – a dog that can kill rats quickly is to him evidently the most wonderful work in creation. It was very amusing to hear him talk in the most solemn tones of the difficulty he had to preserve the peace among his six ratkillers, for sometimes when there are no rats these sagacious animals try to kill each other by way of passing the time pleasantly. Mary W. brings bags of rats down from London for them to kill. He gives 6d. a piece for the rats! Sometimes a rat will escape from his fine dogs. The other day old Mr. Woodford found one in his hat in the Hall!

Mary Woodford played and played well; rather too fast but very smartly and well. She also sang "The Lucknow Leaves," "His Watery Nest," and "Esmeralda." She hasn't much voice but

great great love you can expect here from me, from your sisters, from my dear little girl and from your girlfriends. There are certainly few girls who are loved as much as you are. Knowing this should make you happy although you are so far away from those who love you. You must think constantly about our love.

quite enough to make it worth singing. Beatrice Lake played too - all the Marches Funebres of Beethoven that I am so fond of. She played as near perfectly as most girls. Jessie won't play in society. She does not think she plays well enough and is shy about it, too. I don't know that she is naturally very shy but she is extraordinarily modest about her own accomplishments.

I went into the City on Saturday to try and find something about the Coal mine business. Mr. Farmer, who has the negotiation in hand, was gone. I wrote him a note and shall, I hope, hear something tomorrow.

We have had the most terrible fogs here lately like those you may remember last year. My train is frequently late and very late sometimes.

We go on much the same in Whitehall Place. There is never anything ('new' crossed out) stated. I am told the Secretary has drawn up a scheme of promotion for the office but that the First Commissioner, who is an idle man, is too indolent to give the matter his attention (but this is unfounded I think. I must get promotion before too long). I heard a fine sermon last night from Scarth on the end of the Church's year and the approach of Advent. He is sometimes almost eloquent when he is moved and there is a good reason for a stirring discourse. Next Sunday is the first in Advent.

I spent most of the evening with Trot and had sandwiches instead of going as usual to the Lakes to supper. The Lakes had some friends in so I didn't much mind being away but I went in at 10 o'clock as I passed to say Goodnight. This is the sort of way my life passes.

I have lately read Commander Maude's book British Columbia. Jack's name is mentioned in it twice. It is a record of the 4 years Commission of the Hecate. Anyone writing Jack's life w'd get a good idea of that part of it from the description in the book.

25 Nov. Your dear little letter dated 2nd. Oct. reached me yesterday. It is a great pleasure to hear from you. But your last was the saddest I have heard from you since you left England. I don't know whether it is wrong or not to be utterly indifferent to the World (but I sh'd say it was). At any rate, it is certain to produce unhappiness and, therefore, sh'd be avoided. I mean that state of mind in which one does not care to live. You know as well as possible that it is far from being a happy and contented state – it can only arise from an inward consciousness, perhaps only half perceived, that one has not had one's deserts in this world, and if that is true, it is wrong and shd. be snuffed out. But whether wrong or not, it is so undesirable that anyone shd. face into what is certainly a morbid state of mind, that it sh'd be discouraged in every possible way. I wish you had some settled occupation at Sydney. You evidently want some distraction, to use a French expression. I sh'd rather see you come home at once if you cannot sort out that sort of feeling – much as I wish that you sh'd stay long enough to see whether the climate will set up y'r health.

The flowers you sent were in perfect preservation- the moment I saw them I knew they were daisies and a pansy, and I knew, too, immediately where they came from. I always carry a daisy in my purse from our grave at Crayford. These daisies I shall put in a book. Send some more flowers from dear Jack's grave if you think of it.

26 Nov. 74. The Lieut. Dawson whom you mention dined with Jack and me and Cooper a few days before he left for Australia; it was while Jack was in his old rooms in Upper Gloucester Place. I remember the man well. I talked to him most during dinner and I remember perfectly well that he made a most violent and spiteful attack upon religion, the moment he discovered that I believed in it! I forget whether it was upon

religion as a whole or the church in particular; whichever it was the impression left upon my mind was that he didn't believe in anything, and that he proclaimed his creed as loudly as possible out of bravado and to impress other people with the extraordinary enlightenment of Lieut. Dawson. He was not at all Jack's style of man and I can promise you that had Jack been alive he would not have found Jack's house his home. I remember he swore so much and used such course brutal language during the evening that when Cooper left however he, Lieut. Dawson, felt it necessary to apologise to Jack for talking in such a way before his other guest who was a Clergyman of course. The man is altogether without any breeding or manners and would not be admitted into the society of ladies and gentlemen if it were not that he belongs to an honourable profession – it is hard for the profession to be weighted with such bores.

I sh'd be sorry to think that you or Jeannie shd. have any intimacy with such a person. I am sure if Jack had seen him behave to you in the way you describe, he w'd have cut the man for the rest of his life and my advice to you is to do the same thing.

I have had another portrait taken. I didn't like it much. There are two proofs sent (wh. I have had to return so can't send you one this mail) one very sweet and one very fierce. I call them the Wolf and the Lamb. I shall send a Wolf to Fred and a Lamb to you! The Wolf is not so much like as the Lamb – which proves that I ought to be renamed at once. I have written to ask for another sitting and will try to look less fierce and meek on the next occasion.

I have been having a correspondence with Henry Joscelyne apropos of his sending Alice to Plimlico. The Sister offered to take her free and he demurs at sending her. I wrote to protest and assure him that he exaggerates the Romanising tendencies of the teaching there. He wrote me back the most mournful letter you

ever saw. Said that he was broken-hearted about everything and about this among the rest and that he gave way because he took no further interest in anything (? and wouldn't) try to get his own way any more. Two sheets of wailing – I hardly knew what to reply; but I did reply at last and told him that I thought it was natural that he sh'd be disappointed at being so often passed over, but that he was in the same position as many other Clergy, that he must take care not to dwell too much upon his grievance for that if he did so it w'd altogether poison his life. I am afraid he won't like my letter – but I could not help protesting against his tone. He has had much to try him, and many men w'd be just as despairing but it is wrong all the same to be so. The fact of the matter is the poor man gets no sympathy from Louisa – they are not the least to each other what husband and wife should be. Louisa systematically snubs him.

It has become very cold here. I had to go to the stores to buy a railway rug today. People anticipate a very cold winter.

I had a letter from Mr. Farmer about the Coal business. He says that Mr. Cullen is still sanguine of success, but that the People in Sydney will not leave it in his hands for sale beyond the end of the year. I am sorry that dear old Jack placed it in Cullen's hands at all. There would have been a much better chance of John Lake's getting it off.

I read Jessie the part of y'r letter which relates to her. She will, of course be delighted to correspond with you and is looking forward to your letter via Southampton. I am glad you write to me via Brindisi. You see it allows me, as in the present instance, to reply so much sooner.

When I went to see Trot last night (I always go in there for half an hour before going to Jessie) I found Mrs. Busbridge there. It was the first time I had seen her since I was engaged. I thought she was rather frigid. She evidently quite expected me to marry Louisa. She did not congratulate me on my engagement. We talked a great deal of you and dear Jack. Conny Busbridge is gone to live with a German lady at Trieste in Italy. She is paid £50 a year.

I heard from Annie today. She wrote to abuse me for not sending your letters to her to read. She does this about once a fortnight with the utmost regularity and always contrives to say something disagreeable but she is a good kind old thing and I only laugh at her. Did I tell you that her Atlantic Bonds have stopped payment again?

Poor Jessie has a bad cold and I am not to kiss her because I shall catch it !!! I spend two or three hours there every evening and we generally contrive to be alone. I am afraid we often say the same things over and over again! The more I think of it the less I see my way to be married next year. I am afraid it will be 1876 – a long time to look forward to – but I don't think we ought to run the risk of being abjectly poor as we might be – and then there is the old question of the Furniture.

Goodbye my dearest- this must be the longest letter I ever wrote in all my life I sh'd think! Best love to Jeannie and the children.

Always your most affectionate brother R.S.G.

Please send the enclosed to Fred and tell him that I sh'd have written on a more becoming piece of paper but that this letter w'd hold no more sheets. I come back from a long talk with Jessie. I can't tell you or describe to you what a darling she is- what a perfect mind and heart she has. I am always congratulating myself upon being the first ever to discover such a treasure for I am sure there must be very few such beautiful girls in the world. You must not think that this is a lover's rhapsody merely- I am old enough to look at things and all the relations in life pretty calmly- but I am always falling upon new points of goodness in Jessie. She begged me not to forget to send you her very best love. Goodnight. God bless you darling.

Please tell Jeannie that I think of and feel very much for her altho' I don't write. You must tell her all the news. Is Percy at the school where Jack sent him? I hope Maude is stronger and that Jeannie enjoys better health.

> Fragments of a letter to Birdie, begun about 10th December and continued during the week beginning 13th December 1874

...Mine. Mr. Farmer has written to say he has withdrawn it from his hands. He places the disposal of it in mine till the 31st. Inst. when unless I can show him good prospect of selling it he will withdraw it from the London Market. I have placed it in John Lake's hands. He promises to make every effort to sell it. I sincerely hope he may succeed. I am so anxious that dear old Jack's debts sh'd be paid. Give my best love to Jeannie and tell her I will do all I possibly can for her in the matter.

Mr. Oliver's notice is well written and I suppose he...

...then so as to change the appearance. I can't bear to think of all the misery he underwent here, poor fellow. I had to get up in the night sometimes to light a fire and boil water for soda bandages to put on his knees and feet – he suffered so; and yet he was never cross; no one could be more patient than he was. He was indeed a fine fellow.

You mention having met Mr. Dawson again. I think the less you and Jeannie see of that kind of person the better: a man with such manners w'd not be tolerated in English society, and the people of the north shore must indeed be at a loss for a lion or a hero, to be excited over such a person. I sh'd say he must have got up in manners from the Niggers of Central Africa but he never went there. I beg you will not tolerate a person who has so little respect for the amenities of society.

It is a great trial to me to leave...

You will no doubt hear from her this mail. There could not be a sweeter or more amiable girl. She is so kind and loving to everyone. I sh'd like you to see her stop in the street and commiserate with a dirty little child crying. The child feels happy at once. She is very fond of talking to the little ragamuffins, even when they are not in distress and arranging their quarrels. She is a great ally of the little crossing sweepers and they listen with awe to her little hints... and are rather happier to be refused a copper from her than to receive one from anyone else. She is wonderfully helpful and kind to everyone, indeed has been enthusiastic for the last month about teaching the cook who can't read or write. The cook has lessons from 8 to 9 every evening! It is most happy and thankworthy, is it not? that I sh'd be engaged to one who has a character beyond all praise and what one could have imagined in its extraordinary kindness lovableness and unselfishness to say nothing of her beautiful beaming face and oh how she w'd shout with derision if she knew what I have written about her; for she is as unconscious as a baby of all this and simply laughs in my face if I ever venture to intimate that she is better or more beautiful than other people.

We had a sad Sunday evening – my last at Gravesend. She was in tears the whole time. I am to go there for the Xmas holidays – we have holidays from Thursday to Tuesday during which...

2 Woodville,
Gravesend Dec'br

11th.1874

My dearest Celia,

Thank you so much for your kind letter to me, which I was so pleased to receive; I did not at all expect a letter from you before, and I think it very good of you to have written so soon. You cannot think what a relief it was to me to hear from you. I was half afraid you might be a little bit disappointed that your dear old Wolfie should have chosen such a silly little thing to be his wife; I did not for one moment imagine you would be jealous for I know full well you would consider dear Richard's happiness far before your own. But your nice letter has quite reassured me and I hope you won't mind me writing to you very often and I shall sometimes hear from you, so that on your return to England we shall not meet at all as strangers. I am so sorry dear Celia that your life in Australia is now necessarily such a blank but I am sure Mrs. Gowlland must be truly thankful to have you with her at such a bad time.

Dec.14th. Richard left Gravesend this morning so you may well imagine I feel rather lost tonight. I can't think what I shall do without seeing him every evening and I am afraid, poor fellow, he will be rather dull at first for he has no friend with him at Gloucester Place. This time, I am only reconciled to his departure in the slightest degree by the thought that I shall have the pleasure of receiving letters from him and you must know by experience what a good correspondent he is. I shall not see him again until Xmas Eve when he is coming to stay with us until the following Tuesday morning. I am in hopes the really cold weather which appears to have set in today will continue, as I do so want to have some skating with dear Richard and it will be such a good opportunity. Trot and the boys are coming here on Xmas day to have some fun in the evening and see our tree which will be a very large one; we have been so busy buying and making presents for everyone and a great deal remains to be done before the 25th. I do so wish you were in England and could be here too. I fear you will not have a very happy time. I often think of you dear Celia and trust that much brighter times are in store for you; you may be sure we shall all think of you specially on Xmas day and long to have you with us.

I don't think there will be as many dances this year as there were last year; the Rosherville dances have recommenced and the company we hear is a little more select. There will be no Yacht Club dances, but the Bachelors of the town propose giving a dance, which, I suppose, will be rather a swell affair for Gravesend. I hope I shall be away when it is given though, for I have been to two dances without Richard and I do not care to do so again.

I do not know whether Richard described the rings he gave me to you. They are such jolly ones. The ring, a gipsy one, is set with a splendid diamond in the centre and a ruby on either side. Everyone admires it tremendously. The second one is a broad gold band with "Myripeh" raised on it; it will do capitally for a guard in the days to come!!

Are you not pleased to hear such wonderful accounts of Percy and Harry's doings at Epsom? I do hope that Mr. Whitcombe will be persuaded to send the latter to Winchester where he would doubtless obtain a scholarship without any difficulty.

Mamma, I am happy to say, is downstairs again at last after having kept her room for nine weeks; she is looking wonderfully well but can only move about with difficulty. I often go and spend the evening with Trot for she gets so dull sometimes; however I think she is looking and feeling much better.

Baby is a sweet mite and grows now beautifully. I am sorry to say she is still unbaptised but I do hope before Xmas she will be Christened.

I hear from Richard his rooms in Gloucester Place are so miserable and look so dingy and dull. I suppose it is after Mrs. Curtis's comfortable little rooms. I am just going to write to him so I must say goodbye to you or I shall miss the post.

Fondest love from your ever loving

Jessica K.Lake

Mamma and sisters send their best love. I enclose Harry's photo for Trot. You talk of being home for the wedding; when it will be I don't know but Richard and I both hope that by some good change of fortune it will be next year; I do hope I shall make him a good little wife; he is so good himself that he ought to have no worries; and he does not half know what a stupid little thing I am and I am so fearful lest I should disappoint him in the smallest degree; you must tell him not to spoil me too much!! I am quite of the opinion that I am the happiest girl in the world. J.K.L.

> 57 Upper Gloucester Place,
> NW.
> 29/12/74

My darling Birdie,

Christmas is over and done, and I am just come back to my rooms after spending the Christmas holidays at the Lakes, and

this is the first opportunity I have had of sitting down to write a letter since I wrote to you on Xmas Eve the letter which you will have received via San Francisco.

And now for an account of my proceedings. On Christmas Eve Jessie and I and Mary and two or 3 of the Lake children went to Trot's to spend the evening. We made a Christmas evening of it with the old round games for nuts, which you remember so well. We came home about 11. I spent half an hour at the Lakes, during which they were all engaged in giving the finishing touches to all the preparations for Xmas – the house being in that general bustle and confusion up to the last moment of going to bed which seem inseparable from a Christmas Eve in an English household.

We went to the little waterside chapel, St. Andrews, to the early celebration and you may be sure I thought a great deal about you. There were very few people there, and Trot tells me that poor Mr. Scarth, who is an excellent man, is heartbroken at the lukewarmness of his congregation.

We were much disappointed to find it thawing all Christmas day, for we had hoped for some skating and another day's frost w'd have made the ice strong. We all went to Matins to Holy Trinity and I took a walk afterwards with Grant my old fellow lodger at 11 Williams Rd. At 3 we had dinner. We were twelve. Mr. and Mrs. Bradley (Mrs. Lake's parents), Mr. And Mrs. Lake, Maude, Mary, Jessie, Kathleen, Amy, Bessie, Nelly and myself. The two youngest and the baby came in to Dessert. We had, of course, a grand dinner which, with the subsequent smoking and pulling of crackers, lasted till 7 when Trot and her 4 boys came in for the Christmas tree. The tree was quite a secret from the children and therefore a great surprise. It was splendidly done. The three elder girls had done it all. (I sh'd have mentioned that at Breakfast everyone's plate was filled with presents, and when the post came there were about 30 letters with Xmas cards and good wishes for everyone. I rec'd a silver mounted pipe from Mrs. Lake, a watch and cigar stand, very pretty, from Jessie and Xmas cards from all the family. Jessie had a set of coral ear-rings and pendant from me, a silver Egyptian necklace and ear-rings from Cooper and a turquoise ring from Annie). Well there was much excitement during the distribution of Xmas tree presents. I had no end of things from everyone, quite a Portmanteau full! and the whole thing was the greatest success. Then we went to the Drawing room and danced till nearly 11 when there was supper and after that Trot departed and we were all in bed before one o'clock.

I was delighted to find the next morning that it was freezing and after breakfast, Jessie and I and the two boys, Harry and Percy, set out to skate. We found a pond that w'd bear and skated for a couple of hours. Jessie had never been on skates before. I took her in hand and before we left the ice she was able to skate alone without falling and the whole time she had not a single fall. I thought that was a triumph of instruction.

An unfortunate thing happened while Trot was walking with Willie and Arthur down to see us skate. Willie in sliding along the road slipped, fell and broke his arm. He is going on very well, but his arm will be in splints for a month or 6 weeks.

On Sunday we went to Holy Trinity in the morning . After Ch. and early dinner I went off to Higham to skate and skated till 4, walked back 5 miles in time for church.

On Monday, the frost continuing, Jessie and I went to Higham and skated on the canal. Many people, however, came over from Rochester and I did not think it safe, so at 12 o'clock we went up to the Sturts and skated with Beatrice Lake (the Mayor's daughter) and Katie Sturt till luncheon time after wh. we all drove off to a large pond about two miles off and skated there till nearly 5 o'clock – it was a glorious day and the ice was good and we had it all to ourselves. Jessie made good progress and I greatly astonished the watchers by my figures. There was really not a good skater either there or on the canal but myself and skating is just the only thing I can do well.

So ended my holiday – it was very pleasant – but today I came back to town. I am in desespoir that I cannot be married next year. It seems so long to wait – but none of the Lakes show any interest or enthusiasm or disposition to help me so that I must wait until I can help myself. Jessie tells me that they all think it very ridiculous that we sh'd be so fond of each other and write to each other so much. There is not much heart in the step mother - and she guides her husband, who is the most good-natured but weakest man in the world. They are all distinctly jealous that Jessie thinks most highly of me and loves me better than her own family. I suppose that is perfectly natural, but it is also perfectly natural that a girl sh'd love her lover better than all the world beside. Goodnight my darling Birdie.

New Year's Eve. 11p.m. I have just come in from skating by torchlight on the ornamental water in Regent's Park. It sounds very picturesque and so it looked. There were not many torches but enough to light up a dark night. We ought to be used to the darkness of the time. There hasn't been a gleam of light all day – one of London's blackest fogs hanging over us all day. I turned out to post a letter at eight o'clock and seeing a quantity of lights flitting over the ice, I came back for my skates and went on for a couple of hours and made myself warm for the first time today almost – the cold here is most exceptionally intense. Mrs. May, who has just been up, says she doesn't remember such cold. Altogether it looks as if we are in for one of the old fashioned hard winters. So the old year lies a-dying. It has been the saddest year since it has swept away the brightest and most useful life in the family. His loss is to me greater every day – I never felt that about any loss before. Compare the danger of his accident with that of two men wrecked in the Bay of Biscay in an awful storm,

which lasted for three days and three nights. They were clinging
to a broken raft without food or drink all that time and were
picked up and saved. The La Plata went down at noon on
Sunday and these men were in the water till noon on Wednesday.
How mysterious indeed to our imperfect vision is the thin
dispensation by which one is taken and another left.

Younghusband was here last night to dine with me and we
talked much of dear old Jack. He said he never since he grew up
had such a feeling of attachment upon short acquaintance
towards any man as towards Jack.

I wish you would send me one of the Portraits of him wh.
you sent to Trot by the last mail. There is a sad absorbed
expression on the face but it is a very pleasant portrait of him. I
always think on this day of that Ode of Tennyson in "In
Memoriam" "Ring out the old, ring in the new, Ring in the
happy bells across the snow, the year is dying let him go, Ring
out the false ring in the true." There is another line (and the rest I
forget) which is applicable to ourselves: "Ring out the grief,
which saps the mind, for those which here we see no more." I
remember 12 years ago when I was spending New Year's Eve
alone at Tours. I copied out these verses to send to our dear
mother. It is curious how year after year the mind returns to the
same thoughts.

I have just rec'd a long letter from Annie. She has been
spending Xmas at the Wheelers. The old Rector Harding is
departed and a new Rector is in his place. The new man had an
early and late celebration and another early celebration on
Friday two days afterwards so that it is fair to presume that that
there will be a little life infused into the Parish.

I had a long letter this morning from my dear little Jessie –
she has been skating since I left but didn't get on so well as no
one could make her skates tight enough for her. She uses yr old
skates wh. you left with Trot – they are too long for her but do

very well. I am going to try to go down early enough on Saturday to give her another lesson.

Well good night my dearest Birdie – this is a desultory letter! I wish you with all my heart a happy new year. May every blessing attend you.

Jan. 11.75. Your letter of the 30th. Nov. via San Fran'sco arrived at my office today. I am sorry to hear that I missed writing to you so often when J was drowned. I really didn't know that I had been so remiss. Is it possible that I sent the letter to Wagga Wagga? No dear, indeed, I don't consider the Australian correspondence a "burden" and you ought to know me too well to think such a thing, but I suppose you were naturally disappointed at not hearing and so couldn't help scolding me. As for sending yr. letters round to the family to read, I have sent all the letters that didn't contain anything at all private. I'm quite tired of receiving scolds from Annie and Trot for not sending them yr. letters when I have, in fact, sent them all the letters you wd. care for them to have – but I am not going to waste my paper in arguments on this trivial matter.

I came up today from Brighton where I have been spending Sat. to Monday with Cooper to see the last of him before he departs for Egypt. He is by this time in Paris on his way thither and will spend 6 months at Cairo and in the Holyland. He seems to think no more of going to Egypt than I do of going to Gravesend. Most of his packing was not done when I left Sussex Sqr. this morning and he was going to leave England at 1 o'clock for five months!!! His mother does not seem to mind his going.

I am so sorry to hear that you have not been well. I'm not surprised that the great heat has prostrated you, but I still hope to hear that in the end it has invigorated you. I am also not surprised to hear that Jack's old friend – he always said that Oliver was the best friend he ever had and spoke of him in the highest possible terms – is a friend of yours too, and I am glad to hear of it. It is amusing that Jeannie's one idea of a man's being civil to a woman is that he must be wanting to marry her. I always think that is such a mean view to take of a kindness or attention offered in the best spirit – and a view which no woman has any business to take until things have gone unmistakably far. The last thing I heard was that (it was) that poor creature Dawson you were to fall in love with, but happily he is engaged and so we shall I hope hear no more of him.

I have just come back from Euston Station (8 p.m.) whither I have been trudging with a large packet of clothes for Fewcott. Louisa wrote to tell me that she was in difficulties about the boys' school outfits so I have sent her down all the spare garments I have been able to find – this is the second parcel that has gone down this Xmas. Poor Henry continues in a very bad way. His fever does not much abate and he has as well a large abscess coming under his arm. I am afraid it will be weeks before he is able to get up. He is still too weak to raise himself in bed. It is a great trial for poor Lou and the sitting up all night will I am afraid quite wear her out. She says all the people round about have been very kind. Lady Peyton has taken two of the children and a Mrs. Fortescue two others while Henry remains in such a precarious state – and every one in the neighbourhood has sent them presents of game and Port and Champagne for the invalid – more than he can get through. I hope they will follow it up when he gets well with a living.

It is a week since I have seen Jessie, but it seems much longer. She writes to me every other day. She used at first to write every day, but the Pere et Mere stopped that as being silly and extravagant!! Extravagant of time of course and not the postage! I have quite made up my mind that now we shall not be married till '76 and indeed then it seems unreasonable for I may not have saved enough to furnish a house decently and unless the

Treasury speedily do something for us, I shall be having only £300 a year and that is really not enough to live upon.

So you see the future does not look very bright – that is to say the immediate future which is that part of it we all dwell upon most, because no one believes much in the far-off future – and yet it w'd be just as reasonable to build one's castles in the air as having existence in '86 as in '76. It is odd that we think we can foresee the plan of next year but shd. think it almost profane to map out a year ten years hence. I have come to the conclusion that patience is one of the great secrets of happiness – depend upon it we all forget that precious virtue. Time the "Enemy" as old Jack used to always call it, may be made Time the Friend – and if we don't make him our Friend we are wasting our time altogether. Time my dear Birdie is the Philosophy – to lug in a fine word – begotten of hope deferred!

Trot's quite well I believe and very proud of her boys. They have quite driven out reminiscences of the Queens College of wh. we hear no more. Trot can tell you as much about Epsom as the Headmaster and does not hide her knowledge under a bushel!

Goodbye my dearest Birdie – give my love to Jeanie and the boys. Tell Fred I am expecting to hear from him again some of these days, of course he doesn't take much interest in all of us. I am sorry the Coalmine c'd not be sold. It was taken out of my hands as soon as I had got John Lake to work upon it – it having been disposed of in Sydney Mr. Farmer told us.

As always your very affectionate brother,

R.S.Gowlland.

1875

.

Fragment possibly written
in January 1875

…wrote to you. I wish we were only a penny post and a daily one from each other and then I w'd often shoot off a letter for you. I had a letter from Mrs Busbridge today and she told me to send her love to you.

Have you heard Laura is engaged…Poor Trot is very ill again with Pleurisy; can't move and is in great pain; she sent her love to you and hoped you were quite well and happy. I spent all the time I could with her last Saturday and Sunday when I was at Gravesend. I went to a dance there at the Mayor's. Jessie was not allowed to go, as the father had quarrelled with the uncle. Curious family they are, perpetually jangling with each other – and Jessie's home is not a bed of roses by any means for Mrs Lake seems to make it her business now to be down upon her stepdaughters from morning till night. This kind of thing goes on to such an extent that I told old Lake last Sunday that I sh'd like to be married in the Autumn. He didn't much seem to like it, said Jessie was too young and all that sort of thing but finished by promising to think about it and give me a reply soon. I shall hear I suppose next Saturday when I shall see him next.

Next week I am going to Vienna – on business for my office in connection with the new Embassy House there. I shall be away some 3 or 4 weeks I expect so if you do not hear from me next Mail you will guess the reason.

I had a letter from Louisa the other day. She said she and her family were for a wonder all extremely well and Henry as well as could be expected: but he is unable to take more than the Fewcott duty.

I saw Peter today in the City and he asked me to tell you that he wished you every happiness in your new life. He was just going to ride with his two children to Brighton: he, and his wife, two children and two servants mounted on 6 horses. He seems to delight in these expeditions and they must be very pleasant.

Goodbye my dearest Birdie – my best love to Oliver. Believe me always your affectionate brother

R.S.Gowlland.

57 Upper Gloucester Place. NW.
London

8 Feb. 75

My own dearest Birdie,

Your golden monogram paper with the golden news beneath it has arrived and made me very happy. If I had not known so much of Oliver and had not heard so much good about him I have no doubt I w'd be much frightened – but knowing what a good fellow he must be I heartily congratulate you upon acquiring such a lover and, prospectively, such a husband. It is for my peace of mind a great blessing that you are engaged to the one man in all Australia whom of all others I have heard the most about. I pray you may always be very happy – I sure you will in every way be more happy when you are married than you have ever been before, assuming as I must and do assume that there is perfect sympathy between you and your husband. And here I ought to say that it is certain such sympathy sh'd exist to a great extent even before marriage. You must not be content to hope that it will come afterwards. I am, you see, assuming what I cannot know. Of course your letter conveys what it sh'd – that you are both very deeply in love with one another, and with a man of Oliver's age and a girl of your nature, such a state of things is not at all likely to change, but if it sh'd change in any degree I only entreat you to reconsider the situation. Don't let "new friends" bias you in this matter. I am only saying to you what I am continually saying to my little Love – "If you don't love me with all your heart and soul drive me away – we shall not be happy without complete and undoubted affection." This must be your guide too – and you cannot be puzzled about it; for to be in any doubt on the subject is to be sure that you sh'd be very careful how you are going on. All this warning will probably be quite unnecessary – but I feel I ought not to spare you it. You do no more scarcely than announce the fact that you are going to marry Oliver without going into any of the details which indeed at that early stage cannot have occurred much to you.

It seems very odd altogether to think that you will probably not be coming back here. I wish Jessie and I were going to Australia. How jolly it w'd be to be settled near you – but one never can tell what will happen. The Government here are perpetually reorganising the Civil Service, like a child who has planted a flower, they are always pulling us up to see how we are growing. Quite lately we have had a great Commission sitting and the report was issued upon the opening of Parliament. It recommended large reductions in establishments and not much inducement to those who remain to be left in the Service. One might go. I can't say – as it w'd postpone my marriage. I sh'd not go if there is any good to be had by remaining.

Jessie is staying in London with an Aunt of hers. I dined there last night. They are pleasant people, which indeed all her relatives are (?and) much better off than her father is. I went to a great evening party (musical) at the home of another Aunt who lives at Bayswater. All the London part of the family collected there – we had a very pleasant evening and I had to face all the relations. There was no one who looked prettier than Jessie – indeed she and her cousin from Gravesend were quite the belles.

You will be glad to hear that H. Joscelyne is recovering. I never hear so I suppose he is going on quite well. He is quite out of danger now and is able to get up for several hours every day. I went down to Fewcott from Sat. to Monday a fortnight ago to see them. He was then almost at his worst and quite despaired of his life. It was pitiable to see his weakness – but that was happily his last bad day, and he has been mending ever since. Immense kindness and sympathy have been expressed by all the neighbours and strong representations have been made to the Bishop to promote him, so that it seems probable that this illness which seemed so disastrous will be the flood tide of his fortune. It is certainly a disgrace that he has been neglected so long.

How strange it seems that you and I sh'd be engaged at the same time! And I suppose that altho' I had a 4 months start of you, you will be married first! My marriage is as distant as ever – the people at Gravesend take no sort of interest in the matter; so I must just wait until by patient saving I can contrive to collect enough money to furnish a house for myself and as the most I can expect to do is to save £100 a year - and that is a good deal out of £290 - you see how remote my chance of marriage is.

You will no doubt by this mail hear from all the girls who will supply their own quota of news. I am going on just as you w'd guess – living in the quietest way imaginable in the room on the 2nd floor here, walking to the office, walking back, reading all the evening – the only excitement a letter from Jessie for I scarcely here ever from anyone else. Then I write to her most evenings. I get through a lot of books in this way and if I only remembered a quarter that I read I w'd become a very sapient young man; but as I don't, I remain what I always was, a very commonplace fellow.

Yesterday was the first Sunday I have spent in London since you left. I went to St. Cyprians and had expounded to me my duty during Lent – for next Wednesday is Ash Wednesday. How time flies!

I am looking forward very much to your next letter with more about Oliver and your engagement and all the rest of it. What does Mr Lord think of it? What does Jeannie and Fred? Did you consult anyone? I expect not. Jessie didn't and she is only 19- not yet but on the 22nd Inst. I am going to give her a locket with AEI on it.

Tell Oliver I will write to him when I get his letter which you said he was going to write to me. I congratulate him upon being engaged to you. He will have the best little wife in all the world. Believe me always to be your most affectionate brother R.S.Gowlland.

My best love to Jeannie I hope she is quite well and all the kindest things imaginable by way of commendation to Oliver. I have been working for Jeannie and got up a great letter for Annie to send to Bp.Eden about Jack and asking him to interest the First Lord (his son-in-law) in her case to secure her the special pension.

> 59 Upper Gloster Place,
> Regents Park NW
> London
>
> 17 Feb. 75

My dearest Birdie,

Thank you for your long letter addressed to all of us. I was much astonished that you proposed to be married so soon. You

were actually married then before we knew that you were engaged. I am sorry that you did not wait till after Lent – but it is rather late to be expressing my regrets at the speed of your movements. I have told you already how pleased I was to hear of your engagement to Oliver and of course you know how much happiness I hope may be yours when you are married – for I am not going to assume you are married until I actually hear that you are.

I have written to you at such length and so recently that there is not much left to say. You will have been receiving two such long dull letters from me for some time past – at a time when you were in no mood to sympathize in the gloomy feelings which filled us here some time ago - that you must be quite afraid of my letters I sh'd think

Jessie is still staying at Belsize Park with her Aunt. Their house is one of the large ones in that road running parallel to the road in wh. Mrs. Bouverie lives – and they overlook at the back the same fields which she has in front of her. I see Jessie pretty often. I always dine with her Aunt on Sunday and walk home from church with them two or 3 times a week. They go to St. Cyprian's or All Saints every day – this evening to All Saints – where (the) Parson of Cowley preaches at 5 o'clock Evensong. I went to All Saints on Sunday morning. The new Incumbent Birdmore Compton preached – one of the most useful discourses I have heard for years. In the evening after dinner at Hampstead we, Jessie, the Aunt and I, went to St. (?)Albans to Evensong. The church is not as full as it used to be.

Annie came up to tea with me yesterday evening to talk about you and your new surroundings. She is very happy at Pimlico. They all seem to like her immensely there and she is so softened and changed in the last year or so that one hardly knows her. Certainly she is one of the best old things in existence. She signs now in writing to me "Your affn. truly single sister"!!!

As for me I am going on much the same as usual, working all day and reading all the evening. There is nothing else to be done. I am in a continual state of anger at circumstances preventing my being married for such years.

Goodbye my darling. Very good wishes from your affn. Brother,

R.S.Gowlland.

I suppose Henry Joscelyne is recovering but I have not heard from them. I had a nice letter from Fred by the last mail and his wife wrote to Trot.

57 Upper Gloucester Place,
Regents Park, London
17 Feb. 75

My dear Oliver,

I'm certain as my own name has become a household word to you so has yours long been one to me and I must call you by that which my dear old Jack familiarised me with. In this very room in which I am now writing did I hear your name woven always with praise, affection and admiration with his splendid yarns. So, as I wish to continue 'Richard' to you, you must let me call you by the name which I associate with this most pleasant recollection of the past.

Thank you very much for your letter. It was exceedingly kind of you to submit your affairs and position to me; I suppose I shall never again – at least not for a great many years –

experience such a pater familias situation. But it is ungraceful of me not at once and at first to have said to you what I do feel very strongly and that is how rejoiced I am that my little sister is married to someone whom my dear brother has taught me to esteem in the highest degree. I am rejoiced to have you for a brother and I congratulate you on having such a good little wife. I have always maintained that Celia was the best woman in the world, but I am now inclined to make one (but only one) exception and so you will easily understand that while I think she is a fortunate girl, I am of (the) opinion that you are a no less fortunate man.

It rather took my breath away to read in Celia's last letter that you intended to be married on the 29th Inst. One of my married sisters is much shocked at the rapidity of the movements – but I don't at all concur. I think if people have made up their minds, and know each other, the sooner they are married the better. I only wish I could see my way to follow your example in this respect – but unfortunately it looks as if I should not be married for a long time.

I am very glad to hear that you have been able to make some interest which may lead to something being done in the Colony for Jeannie. I have been doing the best I could here in order that she might have the special pension awarded to the Widows of Officers who are drowned on duty. There is still some doubt as to whether it will be granted. Such a case does not seem to have occurred before – but I am quite sure that if it is possible to grant it, it will be done. All the facts of the case with the notice you wrote of Jack's life were sent to the First (Lord) Ward Hunt by his father the Bp. of Moray and Ross whom we happen to know and the Bishop says that the First Lord had interested himself in the case and when the papers came before him he w'd do the best he c'd for Jeannie. Then I have been to the Hydro (graphical) Office and all the men there have promised to make the strongest representation to the First Lord when they are asked to report upon the subject; so I am very sanguine she will get the Special pension.

There I am at the end of my paper – I have not said half I wanted and wished to say to you by way of good wishes. You must accept the best will in the world for my words. I suppose there never was a brother and sister more affectionately attached to each other than I and Celia, and therefore however inadequate my words appear (as they do appear to me) to express the vivid interest I take in your happiness I urge and beg you to believe that no one can more heartily hope and pray that you may both enjoy a long life and unalloyed happiness. It will not be necessary for me to tell you to take care of my darling sister – but she is not strong and wants to be watched or she grows careless about her health.

I hope my dear Oliver that we shall be correspondents. I am sure we shall be friends for I have always thought that it would be worthwhile going to Australia to meet you. Dear old Jack used to be never tired of telling me how much I should like you. Well, having used my last margin, I must say goodbye.

Believe me, always yours affectionately

R.S.Gowlland.

57 Upper Gloucester Place,
London NW
19 March 75

My Dearest Birdie,

Thank you for your letter written a week before your proposed Wedding Day. It makes me very happy to think that you are so happy and I hope that you may always be as happy as you have been during the days of you engagement.

Most people seem to find that a very sweet and happy time but I don't think I do. I am always so longing to be married and to have Jessie's society all to myself that I cannot be otherwise than discontented till we are married. She is still in London with her Aunt and will I hope be there till Easter, but there is a tremendous row going on at Woodville and she has been ordered home. I hope however that the order may be rescinded. There was a Mission recently at Gravesend and Maude went to Confession. At the time John Lake did not seem to mind about it, but since then his feelings have been worked upon by Protestant people there and the result is that he is perfectly furious and ill about it – persecutes poor Maude out of her life. Mrs. Lake unfortunately is not fond of Maude and so she aids and abets her husband. Well now they seem to feel that Jessie ought to receive a little of their wrath too, and so she has received scolding letters for sympathising with Maude; and the long and the short of it is things are in a very uncomfortable state – I have even been told by those who know the Parents well that it is even possible that their next move will be to give (?me my) marching orders because I sympathise with both sisters. Of one thing there can be no doubt – Mr. Lake is not a man one can depend very much upon. He is so weak that whoever takes the trouble to try and talk him over can talk him into any moonshine.

I saw Trot the other day. She had come up to town to make some purchases.

Annie I went to see yesterday. She was not at all well – does not seem to be very strong. Dr. Way has been to see her. She is going down to stay at Balham for a month after Easter. Mr. White has asked for your address as he wanted to send you his congratulations on your marriage.

I am very glad to hear that Oliver means to come over to see us here some of these days – it is my only chance of seeing you again I suppose – for it hardly likely that I shall ever leave my office now.

Your account of Jack's boys is not very encouraging. I am afraid they will turn into very rough fellows if some strong-minded man does not take them in hand. I suppose Jeannie has no idea what she will make of them.

Goodbye my dearest Birdie. My best love to Oliver – and my best love to you from your very affectionate brother, R.S.Gowlland.

57 Upper Gloucester Place
NW.
15 April 1875

My dearest Birdie.

Many thanks for your letter from Fairfield of the 9th of February. I am beyond measure, if that be possible, rejoiced to know that you are so happy. This is the first letter I have written to you since I really knew that you are married. Somehow one does seem to have to congratulate such a number of people on various events that when one does want to burst out with something coming from the bottom of one's heart the ordinary phrases will crop up and one naturally rejects them as being trite and commonplace and inadequate to the occasion. But you know well enough without my saying so that there is no event left to happen now except perhaps my own marriage which could give me any soupçon of the happiness which I feel in knowing that you are supremely happy; and I sincerely hope and pray that your married life may always continue as happily as it has begun. I can scarcely realise it at the present time; and suppose I never shall until I see you with your husband. It seems very cruel that you must be at the other side of the globe – a kind of caprice of nature that you and I sh'd be destined to live so far apart.

While I think of it let me tell you a little news I heard today. Your old friend Mr. Ridsdale, the Parson, of Folkestone, is engaged to be married to the eldest Miss Woodward, daughter of the Vicar of Folkestone. Were you not at school with her? And was not your opinion of her rather the reverse of the highest? I wish you w'd tell me what you remember of her. Coates who is a great friend of Ridsdale (they compose and jointly edit masses together – the musical part I mean) wants to know about her. I was rather astonished for I always thought that Ridsdale was and ever meant to be a rigid Celibate. I suppose he found life at Folkestone too intolerably dull to lead for ever alone.

Your wedding was announced in yesterday's Times. I send you a copy of it by this mail.

Since I last wrote Jessie is forced back to Gravesend. The atmosphere there is dreadfully disturbed still in consequence of Maude's high church tendencies. Poor Mr. Lake lashed himself into a frenzy on the subject and pours his wrath upon everyone who does not agree with his ultra Protestant views. I am afraid to go down there for they seem to do nothing but talk folly from morning to night about religion and the advance of "Popery" in the land. Trot tells me that it will be necessary for me to carefully hide my opinions or I shall be told I cannot be allowed to marry Jessie!! Pleasant state of things, isn't it? Of course I have heard regularly of all the proceedings; I never was more disappointed in any man than Mr. Lake; it has worried me beyond measure. Jessie has been commanded to give up all bowing and scraping and "ritual humbug"! To go to Mr. Grant's church is to be followed by expulsion from house and home. Jessie is not to go to see her aunt Mrs. Wm. Lake because she is a friend of Grants

Edith Maude Lake

Mary Neanie Lake

Jessie Katharine Lake

Henty Lake (?) died at school

(and so on). Very painful for poor Jessie. Everyone in the house has to take sides against Maude, and as Maude is away Jessie has to bear the brunt of the battle.

I hear nothing of Trot or Annie or Louisa so I have really nothing to add to this very cheerless letter. I want to send you some small thing by way of a wedding present. You haven't I think any ivory backed brushes so I shall send you out a pair with y'r initials on the back. I dare say they will arrive long after this.

Give my best love to Oliver and believe me dearest Birdie always your very affectionate brother

R.S.Gowlland.

Trot tells me she has heard from you; her letters via Brindisi dated 9th and 15th February arrived before mine dated the 9th. Thanks for the photographs. I think you look thinner than before you left and more like Louisa and Jack than I have ever noticed you looked before. I send you a photograph of me taken in November which everyone scoffs at in consequence of the supernatural "meekness" of my looks.

Henry Joscelyne is sufficiently well to take his Fewcott duty again. Louisa and the rest are well.

12 Whitehall Place SW.
28 June 75

Dearest Birdie,

I reopen this letter to thank you for your's of 7th May which I have just received.

Of course I haven't so much to say to you now that you are married, simply because the thousand and one instructions and directions which it was my business to you in loco parentis find no place in my correspondence and that is quite sufficient to account for the diminished sheets.

I have written to Alick (I suppose I must use your diminutive) about his kind letter via Suez a long time ago. I have, as he will tell you, quite abandoned all idea of emigration. I have just been appd. to? Horel Bridge, wh. I shall keep till I am promoted, so my salary is not to be lightly thrown up and (? I do not doubt whether to take it) for all in all England is the best place to live in. You must make your fortunes and come over and live here. Beside Jack always said that it was only cheap for a bachelor in Sydney – and I shall be a married man I hope in a couple of months. You and Jessie must then set up a regular correspondence - we will have a list of all the mails for the quarter framed and glazed and hung in a conspicuous position so that we may never miss one – for although my letters may not be so long as they used to be during yr. spinster days, I have no notion of ever lapsing into the sort of relationship one has with say Louisa or Fred. That I hope is quite an impossibility for us.

I am just sending you by P & O a pair of brushes by way of a very mild wedding remembrance. I went to the shop and told them to engrave C.G. on them; it was only some time after I left the shop that I rushed back to correct it.

Adieu my dearest sister. I wish you were here, for altho' I haven't said so and altho' I have the dearest little sweetheart in the world, I miss you very much indeed.

Much love from yr. very affectionate brother

R.S.Gowlland.

4 August. Your letter of the 6th of June reached me the day after I wrote the foregoing. I am rejoiced to have good news of you. You don't say whether you are as pale now as you used to be

here. I always think that you look unlike yourself as well as very much slighter in that last photograph you sent us. I wish you would get another one taken. You haven't sent us a sketch of y'r new house yet. I should also very much like to have a large Photograph of you and one of Alick to frame and hang up. Companion ones to that nice Photograph I have of dear old Jack. I think one ought to have one's dearest friends before one and not buried away in an Album. I will send you a great big portrait of me and one of Jessie as soon as ever we can afford to have them taken; but you must, having regard to all circumstances, have patience.

You don't know what a pleasure it is to me to read your letter. Do you know, my Birdie, you write uncommonly good letters. You always wrote good ones, but I think they are better than they used to be. The result of being married? Is that it?! No doubt. Does Alick make you read books? Or do you read books without being made? It is a very curious thing to say but I can't make out how it can possibly pay to write or print books. One simply never meets anyone who reads anything but the newspaper. As for women here, the Exchange and Mart is quite the outside they attempt, if you deduct Anthony Trollope and Company's milk trite productions. I hope very much I shall be able to get Jessie to read a little when we are married. She is not allowed to do so at home – is only allowed under silent protest expressed by parental frowns and ejaculations of contempt at such a paltry occupation!! The result is she hasn't read anything – she has been brought up to believe that "to sew" "to put things away" is the mission of women upon Earth!

I am sorry to hear that poor old Fred's wife behaves in such an odd way. What can be the meaning of it? I don't like her face in the Photograph. It is so common – there is no refinement or softness or feeling in it, if it is fair to say so much from a mere portrait. I think Fred is unwise to let her go away so much if he cares to have her at home. I haven't had a letter from him since he wrote to me from Sydney after Jack's funeral.

The skin you speak of sending will be very acceptable. Many thanks to Alick for it. It will have a post of honour in my new drawing room. I will certainly attend to your orders from Thierry as soon as the last arrives. I will enquire from the Girls who are knowing in such matters, who is the best man, if not Thierry, to go for the boots.

Behold such a long gossip I have sent you! Before it reaches you I shall be enrolled in the Band of Benedicts, so you may forthwith fill the flowing bowls and quaff a bumper to the new Sister-in-law and I know that there is no one in all this world will wish us happiness more heartily than you will.

Much love to yourself and Alick from yr. affectionate brother

R.S.Gowlland.

I think I had told you that 14th of Sept is the day fixed for our wedding. The Sister Superior said it was Holy Cross Day and therefore (wherefore?) admirably adaptable for the purpose. It was a very icy and growly letter.

All among the rocks at Ilfracombe, Devonshire, with a fine seaview on all hands and my little wife in the foreground in a black chip hat, red ribbon, black feather etc. etc.

20 September 1875

My dearest Birdie,

Thanks for your last letter enclosing account of the debate on the proposition to give Jeannie a pension and abusing me in no measured terms for not writing to you such long letters as I did used to in the days when you were a blushing maiden. But you mustn't scold – you know very well that a man and a brother (hardly indeed a lover) can't keep up a correspondence even with his dearest sister at perpetual high pressure. It wouldn't be natural if I did – and I never mean that our relations shall be forced or artificial so that I shall not make any apology at all but assure you that you are not going to scold me into a bad temper. I have no doubt by the time this reaches you, you will be in the highest degree angry at receiving no letter from me for so long a time. I haven't had the time to write! Isn't that a lame excuse – well, I haven't really felt equal to sending you a doleful letter as I couldn't send a cheerful one (all the preliminaries of our marriage were so very provoking) I didn't write at all – but I took care that you sh'd hear from Annie and Trot. And so here we are, Jessie and I, married a week and not yet pretending to be otherwise than extremely happy. I wonder now that we were not married much sooner and I am most thankful that we did not allow it to be deferred till next year. My dear little wife is more beautiful in all her sweet amiable disposition each day that I know her better – it is most certain that one must either be much happier or very anxious for the future after so short an experience as ours has been of the married state. Well I can truly say that I am vastly happier than I ever expected to be and my sole regret is that we were not married very much sooner.

We came straight down here staying one day at Salisbury. We reached that place at 4 o'clock and had time before it was dark to see the Cathedral and wander about the Town. Here we

are in clover as regards lodgings and comfort and we are beyond
measure delighted at the scenery. I wish I could stamp on this
sheet a faint impression of the view on each side of us – a
magnificent bold rocky coastline and the tops of the hills
covered with green – the blue sea fringed with white where it
dashes against the coast or over the outlying rocks. I had no idea
there was anything so fine on the English Coast. Your scenery in
Westmoreland cannot be compared with this.

I have left to Trot the task of arranging our new house. She is
very dissatisfied with the size of the rooms for of course she and
Annie cannot be got to understand that I am not a very great
swell who will give frequent dinner parties. I have arranged for
most of the furniture and I hope I shall be able to pay for it all
without borrowing. We have a lot of nice presents – over 50.
Mrs. Cooper's was the most magnificent – I received from her on
the wedding day a cheque for £100 with the nicest possible
letter wishing me all manner of happiness. It was tremendously
good of her. She had heard of my furniture difficulties and this
present was intended to help to solve. We are going to spend a
few days with her at Sussex Square before we return to Town.
Alleyne came up to help marry us – Scarth actually tied us up.
There were no bridesmaids & no breakfast – a wedding cake of
wh. you shall have a piece when I can get at it. I am sorry to hear
old Fred is so queer in his mode of behaviour. I wrote to him ages
ago to ask him to return Annie's £10 note (?) from Jack for £50.
He has never noticed my letter. Ask him to send it please. Two
friends of his from Young came to see me the other day –
squatters – they gave him the best character...

...Jessie is sitting beside me – we have just both agreed that
we have reposed upon softer places than that rock and so the tide
advancing & the sun setting and most remarkable fact of all,
dinner waiting, we close this letter.

With much love to you and Alick, who I hope is as flourishing after eight months of marriage as I after almost as many days, believe me always your very affectionate brother, R.S.G.

5, Northfields, Ilfracombe
September 20th 1875

My dearest Celia,

I have purposely avoided writing to you before now because I felt that as Jessie Lake I could tell you little that would interest you, and I was afraid that my letter would become a matter of form. But now it is quite different and I shall hope to often send you a little line when my darling husband writes to you. We have been married nearly a week now, and such a week of perfect happiness it has been, so far ahead of any little spot in my previous existence, that it has seemed like living in fairyland, and I can scarcely yet realize that I am the happy possessor of the dearest and best husband in the world; you who know him so well must know that I could not by any possibility speak too highly in his praise. We have just now found a comfortable seat on the rocks, commanding a lovely view of the coast which is simply glorious; we could not possibly have found a more satisfactory place wherein to spend our honeymoon than Ilfracombe. We have capital rooms here and every convenience in the way of good cooking, etc., so I do think that considering we have not one trivial drawback to our happiness we must be the most joyous bridegroom and bride in the universe. We had an exceptionally quiet wedding, at my father's express desire, and were married at 8.30 am last Tuesday and after a hurried breakfast left Woodville at 10 o'clock. Trot is sure to give you all particulars about the wedding, I suspect, so I shall not enlarge

Kathleen Lake m. Hilder

Agnes Octavia Lake

Amy Lake m. Wasse-Dymond

Elizabeth Lake m. Lamac

upon the subject, which, by the way is not a most pleasant one, for we seemed to have such numberless little bothers continually arising before our marriage; the present is therefore by contrast, if possible, still sweeter.

I daresay you have heard that Maude is now a governess in a school at Rugeley (Stafford); she seems to like it pretty well and has plenty to do but I feel sure she will not rest satisfied until her darling hope of becoming a Sister is realized; she often talks about you and wishes very much you had not left England. How I should like to see your pretty home in Sydney: it must be so very nice to be able to make so many improvements, and to feel it is your own property. In my next letter I shall hope to describe our little nest to you, as yet I have neither seen the house nor the place (Thornton Heath) so it will be quite new to me when we return. It is a very tiny house; our only fear is that we shall be at a loss to know how to dispose of our numerous presents. Mr. Cooper gave me a very chaste and handsome gold bracelet, really I think the most beautiful I have ever seen; this and a lovely ring set with pearls and diamonds from my dear old husband were the only presents in jewellery I received, the others were mostly plated goods, fish knives, etc., etc. Trot gave us a dear little round table in walnut wood, Louisa an afternoon tea service and Annie a sofa cushion, her own work, and some silver. The wind is taking such liberties with my paper that writing is rather a difficulty. How I wish we were within travelling distance of you, it is always so much more satisfactory to talk rather than write. Moreover I am most anxious to know of my newly acquired sister, however, it is something to have seen you for a little time only. Could I have dipped into the future I should then have made many more opportunities of seeing you; as it was we saw but little of each other. Sitting on the rocks although very pleasant is attended with drawbacks and I am getting tremendously stiff. I have almost forgotten to thank you for your last letter with the enclosed photo. I was so very pleased with both and think the letter very good indeed.

Please give my kindest regards to Mr. Oliver and with love to yourself hoping you are quite well,

Believe me to be

Your loving sister,

Jessie K Gowlland.

> 2 The Cedars, Thornton
> Heath, Surrey SW
> 20th Oct. 75

My dearest Birdie,

We have returned from our honeymoon to our little house here. I found a letter from you when I arrived in London – no it was at Ilfracombe and I remember I answered it.

The jolly ornaments and rug which you sent arrived a few days ago and we were exceedingly pleased with them. They are quite the prettiest things Jessie has and it was exceedingly good of you to send her such a handsome wedding present. It will always be a pleasure to me to see her arranging things which come from you. The nice little rug is spread at my feet and Jessie is going to put it by the Piano when we purchase one: that article of furniture being rather a costly and not an indispensable one, is still outstanding but I hope we shall have it before Xmas.

I wish you could see our little home – if the Dining Room were a little larger it would be all we could desire. I took some pains in collecting the things and they are quite after my own heart. All the chairs in the drawing room are easy chairs and each of a different shape – we have no big table but three little ones and one good large serviceable sofa upon which my dear little wife is now reposing, for all her housekeeping ingenuity has been rather heavily taxed in the first week of our domestic life - for we have always had someone with us.

She has shown wonderful cleverness in arranging everything – perhaps it is rather ungraceful of me that I sh'd make the first mention of her as a good housekeeper wh. is after all a poor detail. But you must be tired of hearing my raptures which have been I am afraid quite chronic in the last year. All I can say is that we love each other very much more every day and that I never really thought of all the happiness which she has brought me. Indeed, if it is not wrong to say this, it appears to me that I never knew what it was to be thoroughly and completely happy before; and that our sympathy and love for each other is as perfect as I think any thing that we know or think of can be. I am afraid all this is sad stuff and perhaps I sh'd not say it to anyone but my own dear little Birdie.

We spent I need not say a very pleasant holiday. On our way back from Devonshire – we remained a week at Lynton after leaving Ilfracombe. We paid a three days' visit to the Alleynes and then nearly a week's to the Coopers at Brighton – at both places my Jessica won golden opinions – and I was very proud to see her made much of by my dear friends. They all agreed, and I think it was not said in flattery, that I could not have married a sweeter little girl.

Thank you too for the photographs of dear Jack's grave. I shall send one to each of the girls. You know how much we shall value them. I am very pleased with the Cross - it is right that it sh'd be quite plain – it is just what he himself w'd have liked – the design of the Cross is just the same as on dear mother and father's grave. In the Times of the 18th Inst. there is an account by the Chaplain of the ?Trent of Commodore Goodenough's last days – and I see that he lies near the same place.

I feel rather guilty because I have never written to your husband since he sent me a long letter on the subject of my going to Sydney. It is very ungraceful of me and I hope he won't think me a bear. I have had such a lot of things to do and think about in the last 6 months that I have fallen into all kinds of disgrace – if with him too, please make my peace with him. Thanks for his kind note enclosed with yours and tell him that I quite agree that the married state is "the only existence."

Dr. Adam left your parcel at Whitehall Place before I returned so that I haven't seen him but I have written to ask him to come and see me here.

Now I am summoned off to bed so I must say goodbye. My best love to Oliver and kisses to you my dear, dear Birdie from your very affectionate brother R.S.Gowlland

We haven't found a suitable box for wedding cake to go by this mail. It will go therefore by the next. Please excuse the griffonnage.*

> The Cedars, Thornton
> Heath, Surrey
> 17 Nov. 75

My dearest Birdie,

Your last letter reached me on my birthday. Annie came over to celebrate the festival. I delivered to her your letter and Oliver's. She seemed to be hurt about them. Mary Lake was staying here then and we had our first dinner party. We have had only one since when Coates and Younghusband were our guests. It went off very well. Jessie is a capital Housekeeper and Caterer

---

*   scribble

and makes both ends meet in a wonderful manner. She takes great interest in all the domestic arrangements- gives me lovely dinners every day on an allowance of £2:2: - a week – beef being in these quarters at the present moment 1/- a lb! Yes, this is the kind of information my letters will in future contain, I am afraid. For we have seen no one and been no where and read little since I last wrote. I am putting Jessie through a course of my pet novels just now. She is now absorbed in George Eliot's Romola after having played to me the "Femme du Marin", which still continues to be one of my favourite pieces.

You sent back in the parcel from Sydney half of my old glee "Three Little Roses"; when next you are sending anything to Europe send me the other half. Your little rug has found out its destination at last – it covers the floor in front of the Piano. We have laid in a Piano at last – a Broadwood Pianette at £31:10. – very sweet tone – we are very pleased with it – and I am able once more to practice my old friends Bonnie Dundee and Keble's Evening Hymn.!

I wrote to Fred the other day - the letter will go by this mail I suppose. I have flung a few stones at him for never writing to me. He must be a singular fellow. I can't make him out – but Jack said he couldn't either- and if a genial fellow like him couldn't draw Fred out, it is hopeless for me to expect to do so. However I shall write to him from time to time – it is too barbaric not to keep up some kind of relation with one's only male relative – for the sort of cousins we have don't count.

I really sometimes still think I shall not spend all my days in England at Whitehall Place. Our Office is such a hopeless place - everything always goes wrong and every change that takes place seems to make it more intolerable. It is comfortable enough – but there seems to be as little prospect of advance as ever. We have great promises made to us but nothing is done! A vigorous government might improve the Department off the face of the

Earth - and then Jessie and I would have to consider in what part of the globe we could most profitably employ our energies.

Tomorrow we are going to dine at the Mayor's – it will be our first night away from home since we settled here. I have not yet been to Gravesend, but I shall call upon the Parents in law – haven't seen 'em since we were turned off.

Goodbye my dearest old Birdie. Best love to Oliver and you from Jessie and me,

Ever yr. aff'te brother

R.S.Gowlland

Fragment written in
November or December
1875

...told you these previous experiences.

We have made only one acquaintance here – the wife of a Civil Servant living opposite to us called and she and Jessie have struck up a certain intimacy which I am glad of – for it is very dull for Jessie here when I am away. I wrote to the Parson when we came to say I sh'd be happy to help him in any way I could – he wrote back to say that he would be happy to avail himself of my offer and I have heard of him no more. A more energetic Parson in the adjoining parish of South Norwood enlisted me to teach in his neighbourhood and thither I go twice a week to instruct the toughs of the place in ... and arithmetic. It is amusing and ...

2, The Cedars, Thornton
Heath, Surrey S.E.
15/12/75

My dearest Birdie,

I have to thank you for a charming long letter since I last wrote. I am sorry I put off preparing a letter for the mail till this week in which the said mail goes out. I hoped I would be able to spend part of an evening in a gossip with you but owing to an unfortunate accident my hands have been full all week.

You will be sorry to hear that my dear little wife is laid up. She had a great fright on Saturday – the snow falling from the roof with a great noise – which brought on a miscarriage, and she has suffered a great deal since. The worst, however, is now over and I hope she may be up at the end of the week. But the wife won't be useful for a very long time, and we shall have to spend our Christmas at home. We had arranged to go to Gravesend . I telegraphed for Annie to come to take care of her as soon as she was taken ill. She, Annie, has been relieved by Mary Lake who came here yesterday.

For the rest we have been carrying on much as usual. One of our neighbours, the parson, has called and impressed me to teach at his night school once a week. Jessie is to teach in the Sunday school. Visitors will, I suppose, be our chief excitements this winter. We shall have Annie to stay with us during her holidays, which begin next Tuesday. Xmas Day however she is going to spend with the Sister Superior at Pimlico in order that they may see together the last of Mr. White who has resigned St. Barnabas and goes to Malvern, where his new living is, at once. The Mother Superior has also resigned through ill health and the new Mother is Sister Ellen.

I am glad that Trot has sent me a letter today to supplement my short one. She appears to be more cheerful in general than

she used to be. The great progress made by her boys offers a large field of hope. She may well hope great things from them for they are two capital fellows. Louisa writes to me oftener since I have been married. She and the family are rejoicing over the discovery of an old drain under their dining room the annihilation of which they hope will put an end to the frequent illness they have had in their house. I had a nice letter the other day from little Mary in Berlin. No positive news yet of the Civil Service schemes of reorganisation, but we are told that a Bill will be introduced at the beginning of the Session, and that we shall know whether we are going to stay and be rich or go to be pensioned.

My kindest love to Oliver. Jessie sends best love. She is too ill to write. You will hear from her as soon as she is well. Ever your affectionate brother

R.S.Gowlland.

1876

2 The Cedars, Thornton
Heath
16 Feb. 76

My dearest Birdie,

The news of the birth of Possum was our Valentine this year. We received Oliver's letter from Trot yesterday only one day late. Of course we are delighted to hear all about it and more particularly that the infant is a boy. We have made up our minds that girls are empty futile articles and that the faith of all sensible people should be pinned to the introduction of the largest number of the stronger sex. I am disappointed to hear that you were expecting a girl. This is weak, as you will no doubt have concluded before this letter reaches you. Jessie is deeply interested. Anything about babydom has her fullest sympathy. We anxiously await full particulars about what your baby thinks and says and does. You always vowed you w'd hate a baby of your own, but I shall expect to hear that you have revoked all your spinster vows of that description and for the future happiness of "Possum" we trust that you will cast all your old prejudices behind you without regret.(Can't write with this wretched pen, must adjourn).

18 Feb. 76. I had a great fright yesterday. All morning I was under the impression that I was about to be abolished. We have a Treasury Committee sitting upon us here and there are rumours that very large reductions are to be made in our staff. There is no doubt that many will be obliged to go. From something which was dropped yesterday, I thought I should be one of those: but subsequent enquiry modified my impression. From the position I have made for myself, and the reputation I have with the authorities, it is everybody's opinion that I shall be about the last man to be selected for abolition. One never knows, however, how things will turn out and so I have had to consider lately

what I sh'd do in the event of my having to leave the office. I sh'd get just £100 a year pension. I think I w'd come to Australia – there must be more chance there than here for a fellow – here there is none. I have thought it well to give you so much preparation so that you may not be dumb with astonishment if you sh'd see me paddling Jessie to the shore of your domain. But remember it is the general opinion and is emphatically mine that I shall be retained here and that I shall be promoted. Coates, whom you remember, is certain to go.

No change in our happy life at Thornton Heath. Dear little Jessie has been rather invalidish since her illness at Xmas and I am afraid it will be some time before she is quite herself again. We have made friends with the Parson and his wife – they are commonish people. There seems indeed to be a great dearth of decent people about us – we couldn't have hit upon a more barren neighbourhood than this in this respect. The houses all about us are very small or very large. The small people, who are about as rich as ourselves, are tradespeople. The rich folk will not of course look at people who live in such a small house. I am very proud of our small house; it is very pretty and much admired by everyone. It would be rather heartbreaking to have to sell our pretty things for nothing. If we sh'd take that long journey we sh'd have, I expect, to go round the Cape – awful to contemplate. And I sh'd sympathise with that man who, after a disturbed passage, solemnly expressed a wish that if Britannia did, as he had heard, rule the waves, she would rule them straight. Do you remember a voyage from St. Malo to Southampton – and how I nearly expired! Best love to Oliver and kisses to the baby and you from your affectionate brother R.S.Gowlland.

2, The Cedars Thornton
Heath
Feb. 17th 1876

My dear Celia,

I was delighted to hear of the arrival of another nephew. My only regret is that we are not near you so that I might have the additional pleasure of seeing your little treasure and enjoying a great deal of his society. I can well imagine how very proud and fond you must be of your son and heir! We are longing to hear further accounts of him and yourself too. We hope by this time you are quite strong and well We wonder what you will name your boy, in fact we wonder so many things about him that you will have to write volumes about him before our curiosity is satisfied. I am sorry that you were minus a servant when the baby came; I begin to wish most heartily we could do without them; our experience of them has been most trying; I hope soon to have Trot's Fanny who is such a treasure; Mr. Whitcombe won't keep her any longer so Trot has been good enough to engage her for me. We are still immeasurably happy in our little house; and if possible I love my darling old husband more every day and find it difficult to reconcile myself to his daily absence. We often talk of Australia and at this present moment contemplate emigration if Richard does not get some kind of promotion. I shall leave you to tell you about his office affairs. He understands talking shop better than I do.

Richard has just gone off to his night school. We find one great disadvantage; the parents of our pupils universally manifest their appreciation of our teaching by becoming faithful followers! And seem to delight in reminding us of their fidelity.

Mrs Alleyne had another little daughter the other day, the 4th Mary. It is to be named Rosalie Gabrielle Marie; they are very disappointed at having another girl; Mrs. Alleyne consoles

herself by saying there is no succession to the throne depending on it.

We find everything frightfully expensive here, mutton 1/- a pound, rump steak 1/6; vegetables too are almost as bad; we hope to grow a few in our garden this year but the garden at present is such a wilderness that we fight shy of having it done up.

We have this month bought a clock for our drawing room wh. is a great addition; the chief feature in the clock is its mercurial pendulum, which prevents any change in the temperature from affecting it.

Annie is in Pimlico this term. She feels herself quite one with the Sisters now that she is an associate; she is always so bright and jolly when she comes to see us that we quite look forward to her little visits.

How I should like to see your wee bairn. Give him many kisses from me and with much love to yourself, hoping that you are quite well again, and kind regards to Mr. Oliver.

Believe me to be

Your loving sister

Jessie K. Gowlland

> 2, The Cedars,
>   Thornton Heath, Surrey
>   SE
>
> 23 April 1876

My dearest Birdie,

Thanks for your letter of, I forget the date, but it was aetatis Baby 8 weeks. I don't know when there is a mail but I must get into the habit of beginning a letter to you whenever there is an opportunity. If one waits for a mail something always turns up to prevent one's writing.

About little Jack. I am very sorry to hear that his mother takes so little care of him. She appears to be a very worthless sort of person. I cannot, however, too strongly deprecate the scheme for sending little Jack to England: to begin with, I decidedly couldn't undertake the responsibility of looking after him. The management of him during his holidays would fall on Jessie. She is neither old enough nor strong enough to do it. I could not think of it for a moment – so much for my part in his superintendence in England. But I do not think it w'd be wise to send him to England on other grounds. Suppose he comes here – he stays till he is 17 or 18 – he may perhaps dislike to go back – but assuming that he wishes to return to Australia and does so, he would find himself a stranger there. His relatives would have lost interest in him i.e. the only people in the world who have the power to help him in life would be estranged from him. You may be told that this is a brutal supposition, but I am sure that it is not only a perfectly fair one, but one wh. would only too certainly be justified by the event. If those people, his mother and grandfather, who wish to send him to England, w'd expend the same amount of money on him in Australia – and Australia cannot be utterly empty of decent schools – they w'd do the kindest thing to the boy. It is most important to his future career, whatever that may be, that he sh'd obtain the interest of those who knew and cared for his father – here his father is quite unknown. To send the boy here would be to send him into a strange land. He would know only us and we are powerless to help him along in life. If his fortune were assured I should be the first to say send him to England to be educated: but as that is far from the case I just as emphatically say, keep him among those who can do most to ensure his success in life.

I am delighted to be the Godfather of your boy. I congratulate you on his name. It is a comfort to have a reason for a name and this one besides has a sound manly ring about it. You may be quite sure that I shall often think of my dear little Godson.

Dear old Trot spent four days with us last week. We spent Easter at Gravesend and brought her back with us. She was very well and in her usual good spirits. Most of the time she was with us she was engaged upon a little dress wh. (? I enclose for your baby). She is most indefatigable in her work and always has some brand new scheme in hand for making money. She appears to have quite a large business correspondence. I have never met such a clever contriving woman in my life. She has now quite a staff of assistants to work for her e.g. the Reed girls at Bexley. Annie has been staying there. On Friday she went down to spend a week with the Joscelynes. I never hear anything of Louisa. Someone told me that Joscelyne has now the sole charge if a Parish near Fewcott so it is to be hoped that they are a little better off.

Jessie and I were delighted to receive your letter this morning. We were indulging in a longer sleep than usual as it is Sunday morning (30 Apl.) so we read your letters in bed. Jessie worships babies so you may be sure that you cannot tell her too much about yours. Your present letter deals largely with that subject so I will ?continue it. I am glad the boy promises to be tall. I think it is a distinct advantage to a man to be a good height – as great as it is, in my opinion, a drawback for a woman to be tall. I like little women - e.g. my little wife – much better.

We are spending the morning at home today instead of at church, Jessie being not well enough to go and I being anxious to bear her company. Our church is not very attractive du reste. It is necessary to whip up all the piety one possesses to induce one to go to church at all. The dullest of sermons is not only dull but stupid and pointless and, in spite of elaborate music, a coldness and want of heart about the service which is quite repulsive – we had one service on Good Friday and in the afternoon a service for children. The vicar gave them an account of Lieut. Cameron's walk across Africa! Apropos of Cameron some of the newspapers have had some stones to throw at Dawson whose ?debacle has not yet been forgotten. This Cameron seems to be a fine fellow. I saw him the other day – he looks quite equal to walking across several more continents*

The Livings** haven't yet turned up. Your account of them exactly corresponds with what I know of them from Jack. He used to talk to me about Living, Mrs. Living, "Old Spain" and your husband, only I ought to have put your husband first for he talked ten times as much about him as about all the rest put together. I remember he had a certain admiration for Mrs. Living tempered with something like contempt for her waywardness and habit of patronizing. She used to constantly write to him while he was in England. She also corresponds I find with "old Blue Jackson". I don't think she is at all the sort of person I sh'd like. We shall ask them down to dinner – we can't do more for we haven't a bed which will hold two.

Like us then you have few acquaintances - as for friends - happy is he or she that has one. I (?really) have come to the conclusion that I shall... (?not) make any more friends. One doesn't want friends so much when one is married – my little wife and my little house and garden are society and world enough for me. I rather chuckled to see that Oliver does not read

---

*   Verney Lovett Cameron (1844-1894) was the first European to cross the African continent from East to West (from Zanzibar to Benguela via the Zambesi). There were many attempts to cross the Australian continent during this period. The one in which Lt. Dawson was engaged cannot be traced.

** Mrs Living (Louisa, née Lord) was Jeannie Gowlland's elder sister.

out to you in the evening. Jessie is always reproaching me for my idleness in this respect. I have so long (been) used to smoke and read to myself that it is not often that I read out to her. If I didn't smoke I suppose I sh'd. Our programme when we were engaged was to read all kinds of wise books in the evening together but like most programmes of that kind, this has fallen through. Jessie was to practise a great deal too in the evenings but this has not been realized. She has just begun to have music lessons, and so far there has been more practising than before, but it is a new broom. As, however, my curious little wife will presently perhaps be looking over my shoulder, I must not abuse her any more. She is very much better in health during the last six weeks. Now dinner is announced so I must break off.

4 May 1876. Jessie just off. Am very busy today so can't say much more than that the Livings are at Camberwell - such an out of the way place - I never was there in my life - might as well have remained at St. Leonards! – and are coming to dinner with us on Wednesday next. Best love to Oliver and kisses to Baby. Ever your most afft. Brother, RSG

> 2, The Cedars,
> Thornton Heath,
> London S.E.
>
> 30 May 1876

My dearest Birdie,

Tomorrow I am going to walk to Epsom with Grant to see the Derby and the next day this mail via Frisco goes out. So I think I had better write to you tonight lest tomorrow night may find me too lazy and dissipated to do anything.

I am sorry to hear that you have had such a dry summer all the time that we have been groaning over the cold and the rain and this summer you have been in the condition of the proverbial parched pear. I hope the Heavens sent water before it was necessary to invoke the locomotives. One wonders what the world could ever have done all this time without steam. It is called in to help us through all our difficulties. Where a community in the Middle Ages would have ordained a solemn fast and days of conciliations, your modern calls in the Civil Engineer, or petitions the Local Government Board. Is this self-reliance a key to this so-called Infidelity of the Day, I wonder? But I have no intention of preaching – see where your drought has carried me!

We have finally got into summer and very delightful it is. All the trees are out, the fields covered with buttercups and daisies more than I have ever seen, I think – this is a wonderfully pretty neighbourhood in the summer. Today I left the train at Streatham Hill, the station before ours, and walked through the most delightful lane home, the air heavy with the perfume of the may. It is quite the most delightful time of year this opening of the summer – far more beautiful in every respect than the much praised "Glad May Day" when somehow it is generally snowing! Last night from our windows we could hear the nightingale. I don't think you have that note in the Tropics – for Tropics I must call a climate where you have no rain all the summer.

John Living came to call at my office a month ago: I liked(?) him much. A week later he and his wife came to dinner here – the most affected woman. We didn't like her – perpetually "showing off", quite overwhelmed by the consciousness of her own supreme cleverness and superiority. She seemed very disgusted with England – thinks everything in Australia far better, the very shops in Sydney far finer than those in London! – and so much cheaper. One felt quite distressed to think that she should ever have quitted such a habitation of bliss – and then the grandeur of her father's house and position! We were quite shut up and felt we ought to crawl before the possessor of so much wealth and magnificence. I shall never have the courage to ask her to eat salt in such a hovel as No.2 The Cedars again. She assured us, however, that our house is larger than yours. It was some sort of consolation to know that Australia did contain so mean a residence! She spoke very affectionately of you but one could see at a glance that she was a most untrustworthy person and a thorough mischief-maker. I don't think I ever met a more transparently artificial person in my life. She told us that your husband was "considered" clever but this was in the patronising tone of one who w'd not depreciate our relations more than was absolutely necessary. I am sure I hope we shall never see the creature again. I do detest and abhor with all my heart and soul humbug. Du reste - we have heard nothing more of them.

1 June 76. NO time to add another word.

Love to Oliver, ever yrs. affec. RSG

2, The Cedars,Thornton
Heath,
   Surrey, S.E.

29 June 1876

My dearest Birdie,

We haven't heard from you either via Francisco or Brindisi. The mails have just come in – I suppose you are absorbed in your baby, as we, I suppose, shall be shortly.

We have been having a warm time of it. The summer has burst upon us with a bang so to speak. The hot weather is

thoroughly enjoyable if one is quite well. I don't know that I have ever before so thoroughly appreciated it. I don't know when before I have been so thoroughly well all through the Spring – the time in the year when the joints in one's harness are most exposed. Jessie is looking pale but she is quite equal to a long walk. I expect she will not write to you today. She has had an old schoolfellow, one Florence Freemen, staying with her, therefore no leisure for writing. We dined with the Freemans the other day – rich people having a house in St. John's Wood. I liked them very much and we have half arranged to spend our holiday at Eastbourne when they are there in order to see more of them. There are 5 daughters and 3 sons! The father is sufficiently wealthy to pension his two brothers' widows – the one with £1000 the other £600 a year. I should begin to doubt whether I was a true Briton if I did not feel my heart enlarged by admission into the circle of a man who has "succeeded" so sincerely. Florence our guest is a nice simple girl who is quite contented with our humble ways. We like having her with us – this is rare. We generally prefer to be alone – and however much we like to have people with us we always invariably congratulate ourselves on being alone again.

I don't think I have written to thank Oliver for his kind letter in which he asked us to stay at Shelcote upon our pushing our canoe upon your oyster banks. You must thank him for me. I shall not have time to write today; for we are overwhelmed with work here today in consequence of the distribution of tickets for the Review of 90,000 Volunteers in Hyde Park falling upon us.[*]

The Livings are just gone off to Paris for 3 weeks. Isn't it odd they have taken a house for 2 months with option of staying 3 months within a mile of our house! Jessie and I have dined there

[*]   The Illustrated London news of 8 July 1876 carries a double page print of the Volunteer Review in Hyde Park with the Prince and Princess of Wales passing along the line.

with them and I have since been over two or three times to see them. Madame has dropped a good deal of her loftiness – finding I suppose that it didn't answer with us – and has tried to be pleasant. She has more sense of the ludicrous than women usually have. I can't get used to the Sydney drawl – it is very painful to listen to long. The children are left behind in charge of the governess – they are merry natural little things. The parents work like drag horses at sightseeing, concert, theatre, opera going – they even go a great deal to church which must be the greatest trial to all of them, one would think. The medley of doctrines they must hear! In the morning to Spurgeon, in the evening to the Procathedral, next Sunday a confirmation of Mackonochie & the Italian Church Hatton Garden! One wonders they don't get worn out. Mrs. Living told us she was delicate when she first came over! She works harder & gets through more than any woman I ever heard of. They have been so fortunate as to find a house with a cow and pony attached and included in the rent.

Percy Whitcombe is up for Matriculation at London University. It is important that he shd. pass in order to clear him of several examinations in the medical schools. He is a very quiet boy – grown quite nice looking – and so far thinks he has done very well. He comes in to see me here between the morning and afternoon papers.

Louisa has threatened to come up today to spend a few days with us, but she is so erratic in all her proceedings that we don't expect her. Mary, who has been at school in Berlin all the winter, is coming home for the holidays. Louisa is coming up to meet her.

I spent a Saturday to Monday at Brighton the other day. Old Cooper goes on much the same as usual. He goes away regularly every winter now for 6 months. The 6 summer months he spends in England – only a few weeks in Brighton the rest of the

time in Scotland, Ireland, the Lakes, etc. He always brings back
with him from the East a lot of curiosities – especially costumes.
He has quite a valuable collection of Arab garments. He brought
Jessie back a Spanish Fan and an Arab burnous.

Goodbye. Best love to Oliver and Marcius. I hope he is
growing well and takes due notice. It was very brutal of Fred to
treat him in such an offhand manner! I can quite fancy how your
maternal dander was up!

Ever yr. Afft. R.S.G.

                                        H.M. Office of Works,
                                        Whitehall Place, SW.

                                        7 August 1876

My dearest Birdie,

I wrote to you the other day via San Francisco. I write again
now to tell you about Trot. You know she has for a long time
been in a bad state of health. Recently she has suffered a good
deal from that swelling outside the throat which you remember.
She was last week persuaded to see a private throat surgeon on
the subject. He at once said it was most serious and that she
might be suffocated at any moment, that at most she could not
survive a couple of years if the swelling was not at once removed
by an operation. She determined at once to undergo the
operation. She took lodging in Harley Street close to the Dr's
house on Tuesday last and there at 5 o'clock that evening the
operation was performed. There were two Doctors and two
nurses. It appears to have been very severe pain – Trot fainted
twice once so long and so seriously that the Drs were frightened.
That night of course she was in a sinking state and so she was all

the next day and night. Her weakness seems to have been much greater than the Drs anticipated. The operation consisted in emptying the lump and setting up inflammation in it. This has to be done again and would have been done already had she not been so weak. They are afraid to risk another bad fainting fit. She is now therefore being fed up to meet the rest of the operation. I see her every morning and evening. This morning, Friday, she seemed decidedly better and had much less pain in the wounded part. She is, however, very nervous and depressed about herself and very much dreads the pain which she must endure when the next stage in the operation is reached. The Dr said she would have to be under him 3 weeks but this delay may defer this cure till a later date. All I can tell you about her is that she is making very good progress – but we shall be all very anxious till she is really convalescent which is at present far from being the case.

Many thanks for y'r Letter. I went into the City to get the £15 you sent to the three girls. They w'd not pay it without a draft – you sent no draft. Will you do so? But as Trot's £5 is now so urgently wanted I shall go and try to get them to dispense with the draft if it doesn't come on Tuesday by Southampton. The expenses Trot is put to are enormous – Room and nurse £4:4: a week; her own food will be at least £2:2: more. Jessie & I have had to give up our projected visit to the sea, but we should be only too happy to do a great deal more than that to help dear old Trot.

We have Arthur staying with us. Trot sent off your little clothes by the Somersetshire on the 27th June. I am in great haste – goodbye. I will write by next mail by whatever route. Ever yr aff. RSG

Love to Oliver – I sent his letter to Trot to young Richard Gowlland, who entre nous is a conceited young prig – I don't think he w'd. do for Australia. Fred wrote Annie a sarcastic letter ending "Yours with love and as much £5 as I can spare!" This is the first letter he has written her since his marriage. The danger in Trot's case is that the inflammation which must be set up in the throat to make the outside and the inside of the swelling adhere may not be under control to stop at the right moment.

The Dr. however is quite sanguine and we must try to be so too. It is very kind of you to tip the girls – old Whitcombe won't help with the expenses!!

The Beach,
Brighton.

23rd. August 1876

My dearest Birdie,

Here we are away for our summer holiday since Saturday the 19th. Mrs

Cooper asked us to spend ten days with her at the beginning of our leave and we are

accordingly her guests. We do all we can to benefit by the change of air and we decline to write our letters under a roof. I don't know when I experienced such perfect weather. The sun is shining, the waves are lapping, the while there is a gentle breeze. Jessie is buried in Jane Eyre, which she is reading for the first time, and is going to write you a line presently so soon as the pen and ink are at liberty and I shall have covered these pages and return to a French novel I am indulging myself in. It's delightful to be a gentleman at large and to be able to eat one's breakfast without apprehension of losing one's train to London.

Jessie is my only care. A strict surveillance has to be kept however. She has a passion for sour apples which requires to be watched! But this is her only vice so far as my experience

extends. She is looking pale I am afraid her domestic worries
have worried her not a little. I told you in my last letter we seem
to have found a treasure of a servant at last and are looking
forward to a fair measure of domestic comfort when we return.

We find it very pleasant staying here. Mrs. Cooper lets us do
as we like – as long as we turn up to feed they seem to be quite
happy – we moon about all the rest of the day and even after
dinner were out to see the stars. Old Cooper is engaged over his
books and papers in the morning. In the afternoon he takes a
walk with me while Jessie goes out to drive with Mrs. Cooper.
Such is our life at the sea side. You may throw in a great deal of
tobacco consumed and as much spooning as can be wedged into
one day!

The Lakes and family have been staying 2 months at
Margate. They asked us to go and spend a week with them just
before they leave and I think we shall do so. We have only been
to see them once since our marriage. They have always tried to
be very civil to us when we have been in the midst of our various
domestic troubles – and have generally held out the olive branch
on all occasions. I have come to the conclusion that all their
strange behaviour to me arose from native eccentricity rather
than malice.

I have long had a theory that a sane man or woman is the
exception. Once adopt this healthy creed and your life becomes
happy comparatively. You can endure with comparative
equanimity the otherwise irritating behaviour of the vast
majority of one's contemporaries. If you apply my theory to the
circle of your relatives, friends and acquaintances I am sure you
will be astonished by the truth of it.

I am inclined to think of Mrs. Livings. It would be charitable
to say that Mrs. L was out of her mind. – but I think she is merely
malicious – if indeed she is not sometimes drunk which is
Jessie's theory about her – a more terribly despicable woman I

have never met. She came to see us the night before we started –
and railed against everything English in a way which really
irritated me. She had been making a tour along the South Coast
and had visited Brighton among other places. They were all
"filthy holes". She was longing for the day when she'd leave this
filthy land and return to her beloved "Ustralia" as she calls it! It
was a great comfort to us to think that we shall never see the
woman again. I sh'd cut them at once if there was any prospect of
their becoming our permanent neighbours. It appears to be her
opinion that rudeness is wit. Such a person w'd not be tolerated
for a month in any decent society in England – and how you can
let her inside your house is beyond my comprehension – she
sh'd never come inside mine if they were going to take up their
abode in these parts. It is a little too much to expect that because
one's brother has married into a family one sh'd be called upon
to be civil to all their vulgar relations. If you take my advice you
will give all the pack of Lords and Livings as wide a berth as
possible. What provoked me as much as any thing in this woman
was the way in which she hinted that your new relations were all
common people of disreputable origin who would not be
received in the upper circle of society in which she, Mrs. L.,
moved !!!!! I let her have a little of my mind about her tone of
conversation the last night we met and could see that she was in
an awful rage. That's enough of a disagreeable night.

Poor old Trot is at Folkestone with Annie – after 7 weeks
severe illness she is unable to walk. Her neck is not healed and
she is frightfully weak. She is very much alarmed about herself
and it is no wonder. However the Dr. seemed to believe that she
w'd suffer a great deal from weakness. We had little Arthur with
us for six weeks and only sent him home just before we left
Thornton Heath. He is a dear little fellow and we were quite
sorry to part with him.

Percy Gowlland

How is dear little Possum. We can quite understand your raptures about him. I often think that perhaps I shall see him before I shall see you again – as it is possible you will send him to school here.

Now I must wind off – my best love to Oliver – I hope you are all well and happy – Jessie is going to write I believe – Adieu – Ever your affectionate brother

R.S.G.

44 Sussex Square,
Brighton

My dearest Celia,

Now we are on leave I can have no possible excuse for not enclosing a line in Richard's letter. Hitherto I really have not had time: so many domestic difficulties following in succession have kept me constantly employed. Richard is having a swim he is quite in his element and will persist in going a long distance from land wh. keeps me in a constant state of alarm; I wish you could see my dear old husband: he is looking so well and jolly and enjoys his holiday most thoroughly. We have great fun and much spooning together, as we can do just as we like here. We are glad to hear all you tell us of your little Possum. We are looking forward to the time when we shall have a similar treasure whose praises we shall never tire of writing; the little treasure involves a lot of expense and work and much work with a will when our holiday is over; my delight in the happy anticipation is perfect and I know my dear old husband is equally pleased; what a perfect father he will make; all the people I meet are such poor creatures compared to my darling old Richard that I sometimes wish we could live on a desert island and avoid all contact with his inferiors. Richard has said a good deal about Mrs Livings; we both dislike her immensely although I believe she has made every effort to impress us with her cordiality and general amiability; at times she has been passably pleasant, but she has more often stroked us up the wrong way and left us feeling very angrily disposed towards her. She tells us living in Australia is much cheaper than here, the heat more tolerable, the inhabitants far superior, in fact poor old England in her estimation is a hole that is scarcely habitable and its inhabitants all savages. She tells me that you and also Fred and his wife live in a most luxurious way and have most recherche little dinners etc.etc. We felt quite ashamed to ask them to our humble abode but after all we gave them a better dinner than they favoured us with.

Poor old Trot is very sadly weak. I do not know when she will regain her strength: her spirits and energy seem quite to have failed her. I enclose you a paper from the stores about the watch you wished to know the price of. I am sorry not to have sent it before but quite forgot. There is no room for the paper so I copy it.

The price of a keyless hunting watch with figures marked on the outside is:-

Fusee keyless £35:17; Going barrel £30:15. In silver cases £10 less. All compensation balances.

We have just come in to luncheon and are driving out earlier than usual so I must say goodbye. My dearest love to your dear wee boy and with much to yourself,

Ever believe me

Your loving Sister

Jessie K. Gowlland.

1877

The Cedars,
Thornton Heath,
Surrey, S.E.

7 February 1877

My dearest Birdie,

I see in today's Times that the Hankow, the ship in which the Livings embarked for Australia, reached Melbourne the day before yesterday. It seems to bring you a little nearer to us when one gets news of what's happening in Australia so soon after the event. You will have seen the Livings and heard all about us long before this reaches you. I was talking to Captain Hull today of the Hydrographic Branch of the Admiralty. He told me that Dawson, who is now attached to the department, is living at Bexley! Hull seemed to think that the great virtue of Dawson was that if he hated you he let you know it. He seemed to consider him a very clever fellow. Mrs. Living was anxious to know what had become of Mrs. Dawson. You can gratify her curiosity.

We keep the very even tenor of our ways. It seems that we shall be quite unable to go anywhere any more or at any rate until the boy is grown up. Jessie seems to be his slave. I am surprised that any mother survives the nursing a baby. Ours is said to be of average goodness but he always wants refreshment once in the night and that interruption is a serious break in the night's rest. We can generally keep him quiet when he is irritable in the daytime by walking him up and down and jolting him about incessantly. When he does cry, he does it with a will and, as Jessie says, "holds his breath" between the peels. I am afraid he is an obstinate fellow for he grows almost purple if he doesn't get his way. He will be eight weeks old tomorrow and has grown a good deal since his birth. We have a little nurse for him but her situation is almost a sinecure for Jessie simply does everything for him. The little nurse carries him out for a walk every day and Jessie marches behind. We have her eldest little half sister staying with us now. Jessie went home went home for a couple of nights a fortnight ago just to just to show off the boy. They all thought him a wise solemn looking infant. Everyone is struck by his very big nose.

I went to see Annie on Monday. She came back from Westmoreland on Thursday. She is charmed with Mrs. Sykes and Mrs. Sykes she thinks is equally bewitched by her. At any rate Mrs. Sykes expressed her regret that Annie's visit was over and arranged that she sh'd spend next Xmas at Grasmere.

We are all wandering what will be the end of the Eastern question. We hear today that Midhat Pasha, the Turkish John Bright, is exiled. That means that none of the Turkish reforms will be carried out I expect. I suppose the end of it will be that the Russians will walk down to Constantinople where no doubt they will meet some of our countrymen in red coats and there will be a considerable flare up. Well I hope the P & O boats won't be stopped and my letters to you and more especially yours to me sent to Russia to make cartridges. *

Poor old Trot has had another slight operation. I haven't seen her since but it appears from Annie's account to be very different from the first. She was able to go in a cab to Mrs. Hewitt's afterwards. She seems again to be dreadfully depressed about her husband. He declines to pay anything whatever for her. She fears that there must be another explosion soon; and he is so entirely out of his mind that there is no knowing what he may do.

*Midhat Pasha was a Turkish politician who, as Governor of Bulgaria, swiftly raised that country from penury to relative prosperity. In 1876 as Grand Vizier to Sultan Abd al Hamid, he secured the promulgation of the first Turkish Constitution.

Midhat was subsequently exiled, made Governor of Syria, and in 1883 imprisoned and murdered.

>   The Cedars,
>   Thornton Heath,
>   Surrey S.E.
>
>   6 March 1877

My dearest Birdie,

Your letter of the 14th Jan ! sent via Trot arrived here this morning and was doubly welcome inasmuch as it is a long time since we heard from you. You are quite right to economise your Postage Stamps by making one letter convey news to all the family.

I am sorry to hear as before you suffer so much from the heat. I hope next year you may be you may be more inured to the climate. Has diet anything to do with it, I wonder? Have you tried a milk diet? I mean drinking nothing but milk. Every other liquid is heating more or less. As you have a cow there w'd be no difficulty in getting good milk

The dear little Possum! To think of him giving a picnic in his yacht on his birthday! We laughed immensely over that part of your letter. I'd (?really) like to see him.

I wrote to you last on the 10th Feb ? I probably didn't mention that Jessie had been feeling rather unwell for the three days previous to that. She had a sore throat and had felt giddy but we thought very little of it and referred it to the exhaustion wh. is rather to be expected from nursing. The Dr. came to see the baby on the 12th Monday – he had been suffering from diarrhoea – and Jessie showed him her throat and a rash wh. had appeared. He at once pronounced her to be suffering from

Mary Neane Lake (?)

Scarlet fever! Imagine my consternation on my return in the evening laid up with (? such a horrid) disease. Well, she has been in bed for the last three weeks and only yesterday was allowed to get up. She has been the whole time wonderfully well in the circumstances. She has had the fever in its mildest form and has suffered I sh'd think the minimum of inconvenience. The Boy has not taken it nor have I or the two servants. I have been at home all the time and shall probably not be allowed to return to my office for three weeks longer so great is their horror of any chance of infection entering the portals of Whitehall Place. I have nursed Jessie myself. There has been very little in the way of nursing to do. I maintain that the greatest difficulty of the post in my case has been to keep the fire in all night! I think I who have not had the fever have really felt often more ill than the real invalid: for my constitution seems the whole time to have been struggling to keep it off. I have had sickness and diarrhoea and ulcerated throat (the latter has not yet gone) and have once or twice been quite done up. The Dr. says all this proceeds from breathing the fever-tainted air. I cannot be too thankful that I have not been actually laid up.

Our little man has been much better in the last three weeks than he has ever been before. This is astonishing seeing that he has been in the sick room all the time. Jessie has nursed him entirely through all her fever. He has grown wonderfully and has never been so well and so bright. He is as we think the dearest and sweetest little fellow in the British Islands (I dare not say the Globe). He has been as good as gold all the time Jessie has been laid up. It has been a fine time for him for of course he has had an amount of parental nursing and romping which is not likely to fall to his lot again. He prattles and laughs now by the hour together, never cries unless he is really hungry and is developing all kinds of pretty little tricks. He has beautiful grey eyes - the colour of mine – and has a sweet little knowing expression. I can't tell you how much amusement he is to us – and how devoted we are to him. He is going to be shortcoated* at once so that he may get used to bare legs before he is exposed to draughts. We shall have him photographed soon and you shall have an early copy. I have been occupying part of my leisure in framing a lot of prints for his nursery – so that we are now (?decorating) it with all kinds of scraps and (it) looks as nurseryish as possible. He is very fond of being sung to – puts his little head on one side and is quite pleased. We both sing ourselves hoarse to please him. I occupy a little bed in the corner of Jessie's room and he comes in to me every morning for a little talk and a spoon. Jessie, however, doesn't like the arrangement! She is quite unhappy that he sh'd talk to anyone but herself and I foresee that quarrels are impending over the too much beloved infant! I am afraid that we shall run you very close in the matter of baby worship.

11 May 77

My dearest Birdie,

Your long letter to me and Jessie of the 18th of March reached us on the 7th Inst. We were delighted with Oliver's post script of the 19th and I may say very much relieved for we have had rather a poor account of you lately. We are rejoiced too that you have the wished for girl. I hope she will always be an ornament to her sex and a joy to her parents. What are you going to call her I wonder? How wonderful it seems to me to think of you with two children who only yesterday – the time flies so fast – was repudiating any wish to have anything to do with infants.

---

*   shortcoats were the clothes worn by an infant when too old for long clothes.

Do you remember now how you used to prefer to hate the whole race of infants? Well they are taking their revenge upon you.

I need not say that I was extremely disgusted to hear that Jack's widow proposes to marry again and to marry such a man. I am quite prepared for any folly from that quarter. Poor Jack! I often pity him when I remember the years he spent with such a person as his wife. It is incredible that a man of such talent could have been happy with such a woman for a wife. I will say this for him though – he carefully concealed any regrets he may have had in this matter. It is tremendously good of Oliver to consider taking to the eldest boy. I feel it is much more my business than his – and if I could see my way to doing anything I would – but I foresee that it will in the future be as much as I can do to keep my little family afloat. My prospects are not at all brilliant. There is little chance of my ever having more than £500 a year. However I hope the event which you mention – the widow's marriage – may not after all come off.

Jessie suffers a good deal of pain in her back and limbs: we have hitherto supposed this was only rheumatism after the S. fever – but I am beginning to think it may be something worse and if it doesn't go away soon I shall bring her up to see a Physician. We are still without a servant and she is consequently worked to death. We have to get on with two little girls under 15 and Jessie practically has to do everything herself. There seems to be no prospect of getting a serv't. We think we shall not really engage one now till we get back from the sea.

Whither we go in July. The boy is well except in the eyes. He has weak eyes and all we do does not seem to strengthen them. He is going to be examined on Monday. He will be five months old on that day. He continues to be as bright and joyful as ever. He is a source of infinite happiness to us both. We think him very pretty. He has at any rate a sweet happy little face. He inherits his father's capacity for heavy laughter.

Poor old Trot is still very ill. Her throat is still far from well. There is an abscess formed on it now, which discharges alarmingly. I never knew anyone so afflicted. What a mystery it is – this inequality of the joys and ills of life. One feels quite ashamed of being so happy when anyone is so miserable as poor Trot is. We hope to spend our summer holiday at some place with her this year. Harry came to see us on his way to Winchester. He is a very bright happy boy. Percy talks of trying for a science scholarship at Cambridge. He thinks he stands a good chance of getting one. Lilly Joscelyne has been seriously ill but is mending. Annie is coming to us from Sat. to Monday. The Sister Emily Mary who is our boy's godmother comes to see her godson tomorrow.

Jessie is very sorry not to write to you by this mail. She really has not had time to sit down to do so. She is very happy to hear that you have another little treasure and are so well. How we wish we could have the Possum while you are laid up! I am overwhelmed with work here. We have been more busy than we have ever been before.

My best love to Oliver. Ever yr. affn. R.S.G.

2, The Cedars,
                        Thornton Heath,
                        Surrey S.E.

31 May 1877

My dearest Birdie,

We have been thinking a great deal about you lately and about your two chicks. I hope you are getting on fairly well and are not overwhelmed by your new responsibilities. Now you have the new baby photographed in his little shirt so we may admire her little shoulders. You wrote to me or rather Oliver did after her arrival to enable him to say with precision whom she resembles. I hope that you may be writing to tell me all about her. Our Tots continues to be a perpetual joy to us both. He is the most charming little fellow. It is quite a marvel to me that one sh'd derive such an enormous amount of happiness out of the contemplation of a baby 6 months old. To think that one might have become an old bachelor and have lived and died without experiencing this joy. I don't think the world affords any rapture to be compared to that which I can obtain by looking at the Tots in his morning tub!!! It is too lovely. Poor little man, he kept us awake an hour last night. He was (?livid) for the first time withdrawn from his usual source of refreshment and put upon the bottle. He objected very strongly to this unusual proceeding! It is high time Jessie gave him up. She is grown quite thin and is continually feeling queer. He is too much for her but still continues however to be a small baby.

Mirabile dicta, I heard from Fred the other day. He appears to be prospering. He said he gets £625 a year and a house from the Bank and has a sixteenth share from his wife's family in a large sheep run and the sheep belonging to it. He was anxious about the drought. He was hurt that you had not called on his wife while she was at Sydney. He said you had not been too immobile to call on other people. His wife wrote to Trot the other day.

Poor Trot, still very ill. She is to have lodgings in London again for a time to undergo fresh operations. I am going up to Harley Street this afternoon to look for a bedroom for her. She is coming up on Monday the 4th of June. We hope that she may be well enough to come away with us in July.

Harry Livett is coming down to dine with us this evening. He is second (? mate in his) ships now…His (? parents) have

come to live in Norbiton. They have three children. HL
continues to be a nice quiet person.

Mr Lake has offered to buy a house for us if we will go and
live down his line. I think we shall close with the offer at once.
We shall probably fix on Bexley or Sidcup.

Very best love to Oliver and kisses to the dear infants. How I
sh'd like to see them. One looks upon all children with new eyes
now – Ever yr. affn. R.S.G.

Aunt Williams departed this life last week I attended her
funeral on Monday.

I have just been reading the life of Charles Kingsley. I had no
idea he was such a splendid fellow. You should get and read the
book if you can.

> Fragment of a letter
> possibly written the in
> summer of 1877
> 2, The Cedars,
>   Thornton Heath,
>   Surrey S.E.

We shall not be able to have her* as the house without her
will be inconveniently crowded. I am sure she will be dreadfully
offended. She is one of those people who won't take a hint and
when she is told outright anything she pretends to be very
greatly hurt. She seems to have no immediate intention of
getting anything to do and I (? now) feel that if I don't speak
pretty (? plainly) she will just seesaw between us and Louisa's for
the rest of her days. You will be sorry to hear that she recently

*   Annie?

has lost her best friend Mrs Sykes of Grasmere who died rather hideously from an interior tumour. Old Sykes of Brighton too has lost his wife.

I went down to see Cooper (who has just returned from spending the winter in Malta) at Brighton the other day. He goes on just the same as usual. It is a lamentable waste of a life. It makes one quite sad to think of it. It is quite clear he will never do anything now but wander up and down Europe in search of amusement. He usually spends the winter at Cairo. He is always threatening to go round the world. It is not improbable that he will walk into your house one of these days. You may remember my telling you about his elder brother who leads the life of a recluse not seeing anyone in the Temple. Cooper has long given up going to see him. He was evidently so displeased to receive even his own brother as a visitor. He hasn't been down to Brighton to see his mother for ten years! and he declines all invitations from his relations in London. Before I was married I used to call to see him occasionally and he was always very civil to me. But I hadn't been to see him since my marriage. I went about a week ago and he seemed so glad to see me that I asked him to come down to dinner. He came greatly to my surprise. He appeared to be especially delighted with the Peeps who played at ball with him till dinner was nearly cold and kissed him most warmly before he left for bed. He is a curious person indeed – a handsomer man than his brother and more clever. He took honours at Cambridge and came up to London and read for the Bar but he actually never was called and he never will be now. His rooms are crammed with books. Especially he buys Geographical works and knows more on that subject than anyone I have ever met.

I must now rush off to catch my train where I meet Coates who is coming down to dinner with us tonight. He is still an

Beatrix de Michele (née Lake)   Jack, Geneveve, Maude, Percy

invalid. Trot continues well, I hear. Best love to you and Oliver from us both and kisses to your Bairns.

Ever yr. aft. R.S.G.

Oct 17th 1877

My dearest Celia,

We are back again in our old quarters after a most delightful five weeks at Brighton which has done us all a great deal of good, baby especially. He is looking perfectly charming and has lost the delicate look he had when photographed. I send you a copy of a photo taken a day or two before the one we last sent; we did not consider it satisfactory enough to have more than one copy, wh. we had, thinking that you might like to see it. I am sorry it is so cut but I have had it in a frame for wh. it was too large. I so very often think of you with your two babies, they must be a handful. I find my one Tots requires a great deal of attention – he crawls about tremendously now and most carefully picks up anything there may be on the carpet and puts it into his mouth. I am constantly pin-hunting, much to Baby's annoyance, for he loves a pin! He is a regular mother's boy and clings to me as tight as he can and says "Ta Ta" to everyone who attempts to take him from me. I send you a scrap of the darling's hair – it is so long I was obliged to cut it a little today to prevent it from rubbing his eyebrows. He rides in his perambulator about two hours every morning, and afternoon. We have just had to start his winter garments; he is wearing now a white cricketing flannel pelisse wh. I made him, and a little loose turban hat to match trimmed with white fur, he is so fair that white suits him admirably. He is immediately admired and nurse is constantly stopped and questioned about "that sweet little baby". He likes to be noticed and on the Brighton pier used to play Peep-bo with strange ladies; Trot was delighted with him, she used to take him in her bath chair and make believe he was her baby! Poor Trot! I am afraid she did not stay at Brighton long enough to do her any good, we wished her to come to see us sooner but she could not leave home. I think Richard is telling you all about her plans for the future so I will not trouble you with a repetition. Fred sent us some lovely emu skins the other day – also some rugs and a few oppossum skins, we had never seen any of the former and were particularly pleased with them; he also sent a very handsome rug for Dr. Mackenzie, oppossum skins with an oppossum "neat"?? (as Richard would say) in the centre. I have been dreadfully troubled in the domestic fray lately having found it impossible to get a general servant. My nurse has been very good and has struggled alone since our return from Brighton, but of course Baby and the cooking have been entirely in our hands (I say our for my sister Mary is with me and I don't know what we should have done without her). We expect Louisa here very soon, she was to have come with her baby but we have asked her to postpone her visit until next year as we are a wee bit afraid of the fever still, it would be serious shd. we have it in the house again.

Richard has joined the Civil Service Volunteer Corps. I don't know whether he has told you, he has proved to be an excellent shot, and he is much commended by the old sergeant, who is delighted not only on this account, but because he has such a splendid chest! They want to make him an officer. A new uniform will be required to rise to this honour so I think Richard will decline it. I do hope you are suited with a nurse now. Trot told us of all your troubles. I do so entirely sympathize with you, dear Celia, and always wish when I hear of these kind of difficulties that we lived nearer so that I might help you of this, the nurse's mother has written to say she wants her home! This is a great nuisance as she is a most useful servant, but I do not think she will go until Xmas. I am getting dreadfully sleepy and I see Richard has written a long letter so I will say goodbye. Kiss your little darlings fondly for me and accept much love

From your loving sister

Jessie K. Gowlland

Richard says if you want a lock of his hair you had better ask for it soon or he won't have one hair to send!, i.e. if in a position to do so! I am thankful to say a new servant has appeared on the scene this morning but upon the strength …

> 2 The Cedars,
> Thornton Heath
>
> 22 Nov. 77

My dearest Birdie,

I really think I must have had two letters from you since I last wrote. Your letters are charming. You always tell one exactly what one wants to know and you are not vague which all the rest of my sisters are. I seem to quite know your establishment and the little cares which occupy your mind. The man who advised his correspondent to tell all the details of the household in her letters down to the creaking of a door would have rejoiced in your power of making domestic details so sparkle. I often wish I could keep you equally au fait in the matter of our doings.

I think the care which sits most heavily upon us is the what appears to be the perpetual coming and going of visitors. We much prefer to be left alone. We are always growling at the imminent prospect of some one turning up to stay a fortnight.

We had Louisa and her boy. We are very fond of old Lou but somehow we like to be alone a bit. Now Lilly Joscelyne is coming for a fortnight and after her Maude Lake for another so that we are just going to say farewell to the delight of being alone for the rest of the year – for after Xmas I suppose Annie will be here. Then of course we have to devote ourselves to our visitors instead of to each other and our dear old Tots. It hurts our feelings too to find as I suppose everyone does find that people are not in such raptures about Tots as we are ourselves – and we cannot bring ourselves to feel with ordinary Christian charity towards people who don't share some of our enthusiasm about him. Alas no one does except dear old Trot and while she was with us at Brighton, Edink was really a very happy spock to look upon – she did seem thoroughly appreciative in the direction of the offspring. These are some of our little cares.

The greatest "standing" care which pursues me is Jessie's want of appetite and consequent emaciation. She is quite a shadow. You would see that from the photographs I sent you of the baby and the mamma. She has been better lately though with the exception of touches of spasmic returns and neuralgia. We have had rather a trying time of it since the baby took to cutting his teeth. The 4th has just come through and so we are getting a little sleep again. It was no unusual thing for me to be leaping out of bed three or four times in the course of a night. Now we sleep generally from 11 till 5 after which we are engaged in protecting our hair from being pulled and our respective noses and ears from being bitten off by the combined effort of the 4 teeth mentioned above

I am very sorry to hear what you mention about Fred. I am not without hope though that the poor account of his professional capacity is a little exaggerated coming as it does from a rival banker. Still it ought not to be possible that such a statement sh'd be even hinted at. It is almost incredible that a man in his senses sh'd have been engaged so many years in one occupation, and that one of the most simple to master, without learning the very rudiments of it. All the people whom I have met here who have met Fred in Australia have never tired of singing his praises...

...Bankers. Jack who ought to have heard if Fred was at all deficient had the highest opinion of his business capacity. It is a pity that he did not marry a wife who could keep him at home in the evenings. But I suppose that there are great temptations to become a frequenter of clubs at a little place like Wagga where there is no public life.

You mentioned in your last letter that Mrs. Living had been raving about the skating rink at Brighton. I must tell you that when we asked her what she thought of Brighton, she said it was a filthy hole not to be compared to the Australian watering places and reminded her of the neighbourhood of the Docks* (the low part of the town she said) of Sydney. This I remember very well for it made me angry because it was so obviously foolish and untrue. I let her know I thought so, and she never came to our house again. I cannot regret that Jack's boy sh'd have left her house. Almost any influence must be better than (that) of a false creature like Mrs. Living. I utterly disbelieve in the possibility of false natures being able, with the best intensions even, to do good to anybody.

A friend of Jessie's has a cousin who is going to Australia for his health. They asked me to give him any letters of introduction which I could to friends in Australia. As his family have been very civil to us, I gave him a letter to you to be presented if he sh'd go to Sydney. His name is Freeman. All his friends and relations are in good positions here and are very well to do. His

---

*   Richard wrote 'Docks' but he probably misheard and misunderstood Mrs Living's reference to the part of Sydney known as the 'Rocks', which is indeed in some respects similar to the Lanes in Brighton.

uncle whom we know and go to stay with sometimes is the great stone merchant of London. Jessie was at school with his daughter and they are supposed to be bosom friends.

I sh'd like to see your dear little Possum and that wonderful baby. You are fortunate to have such a good baby and I think I sh'd be delighted with the Possum. He is just what I like a little fellow to be, and I am happy to see that you don't spoil him. Your description of his little ways is beautiful. I can see him holding up his little 'pandys' to be kissed after they have been beaten. I only feel inclined to slap our Tots when he has, in spite of remonstrance and entreaty, entangled his little fist in my beard and tugs with all his might to get it out again. That is an operation which must ruffle the mildest of men.

Trot writes a cheerful letter from Torquay. I shall not tell you anything about her though, for she is sure to have written herself. She does not say that her health has much improved so far. Her accounts of herself vary very much with the state of the weather. I am sorry to hear that the pain in her lung is not gone.

I am very glad to hear that so far "Oler's" book has been successful. I hope all the copies will go off. Is he obliged to send a copy to the British Museum? If so I will go and see a copy of it. Every book and pamphlet published here must as you know be sent to the Museum.

Talking of the British Museum reminds me to tell you that we (ie my office) have nearly completed a grand new Natural History Museum at S. Kensington. You w'd hardly know some parts of London. Some extensive alterations have been made since you were last here. Northumberland House at the S.E. side of Trafalgar Square has long since departed and a broad avenue runs over the site of it from Trafalgar Square to the Thames Embankment. We are going to introduce a bill next session to acquire land and houses extending from the present new Home and Colonial Offices and Foreign Office down to Great George

St. Westminster as a site for new Public Offices. The Strand too is quite transformed at the Temple Bar hard by the magnificent pile of Courts of Justice which is gradually rising on the North Side of it and extending to Lincoln's Inn Fields.

Goodbye my darling. Best wishes to Oliver and kisses to your wee pets. Ever your aff'ate R.S.G.

I haven't forgotten the photographs of Oxford. They shall be sent...

...poems,,,last letter arrived in a dilapidated condition. All one side of the envelope gone. It is a wonder it reached me.

2, The Cedars,
Thornton Heath, Surrey.

12 December 1877

My dearest Birdie,

Jessie says she wrote to you last; so probably we shall have a letter immediately after this has left us. That is one of the difficulties of correspondence with Australia. One never seems to get into an interchange of letters. The mail is always starting when one doesn't seem to have much to say. Your letters are not at hand to reread when I am about to write for I generally send 'em off to Trot who always promises to but never does return them. She writes to us pretty often. I think her general health must be better although she doesn't admit that it is. We do not hear of the pain in her side now which is the worst feature in her case. She speaks more of neuralgia. So I have good hopes that she is better. She still thinks of going to Nice if an opportunity sh'd offer. Dr. Mackenzie is looking out for some one who wants a chaperone in the South of France. He seems to think that that climate would do much more for her than the warmest part of

Jessie Katharine Gowlland

Richard Sankey Gowlland

Sarah Maria Whitcombe (née Gowlland)

Jack (?)

England. Her boy Henry was confirmed the other day. As his Godfather I have been writing to him on the subject lately and he has written to me very earnestly about it. He promises to be a very good boy I think. The other day Mrs. Cowper Temple asked him over to Broadlands to spend a day with her and she writes to Trot that she was very pleased with him. She notices especially his remarkable self-possession. He tells me he has not done so well in his work this term. I daresay the Confirmation distracted him.

We are going to spend Christmas at Gravesend and a day or two with the Grants at Aylesford. You will remember my telling you about Grant who shared Mrs Curtis's house with me at Gravesend. He has just been appointed Vicar of Aylesford by the Dean and Chapter of Rochester. He is very fortunate to get such a good living so soon. He is 3 months only my senior. The living is £900 a year, a beautiful house and garden with field attached. The place Aylesford is one of the loveliest in all Kent. In the Spring he married a girl with £15,000 down and large prospects thereafter. Grant is very anxious that Jessie and his wife sh'd be friends.

Our darling wee pet is going on very well. He grows more charming every day. He has the most lovely knowing little face. We can hardly believe that he will be a year old the day after tomorrow. I waste all the spare time I have when he is awake in romping with him and have to be sternly rebuked often in the middle of the night because I can't resist playing with him. His devotion to his Mammy is unbounded. He clings to her like a limpet! And screams if she leaves the room when some one else is playing with him. But he always expects me to romp with him from 5 till 6 in the evening and shouts and kicks even in Jessie's arms till I take him. It's very amusing when in the evening, I am in one bedroom and Jessie is in the nursery adjoining and the Tots is on the floor, to see his doubt as to which one of us he shall attach himself to. He crawls from door to door, peeps in and looks at me, alternatively gives a little snort of laughter and then dashes off to the other door! He has a tremendous mop of hair – we have had to cut it in a fringe across his forehead. He has a very good forehead.

Annie is still unattached. I am dreadfully afraid she will be quartered on us after Christmas. If she can't get anything to do there is nothing for it but to make the best of her. She complains a good deal of coughs and colds. I am afraid she is really not at all strong. She is going to spend Xmas with the Sister Superior at St. John's Wood where the school is now kept. I am very sorry to hear that the Tot's Godmother Sister Emily is very ill with consumption. Did you know Sist. Pauline's sister Lettice (I don't know how the word is spelt but it is pronounced " Lettias"). She used to teach at St. John's. Her sister is living here and she and her husband are the only nice people we have made the acquaintance of since we came here. We have spent an evening with them and they dined with us the other day. The husband is a Civil Engineer practising in London. If you remember Sister Peters told me about her. She died a little while ago.

Lilly Joscelyne has been spending ten days with us. She has just gone. I am afraid she is very delicate. She is just the sort of girl whom you w'd say never will be strong. She is very like Louisa in all things except her flow of conversation! They differ much in this particular for whereas Louisa has always something to say Lilly never opens her mouth. She appears to be quite content to sit still and smile at anything said to her. She takes a cheerful view of life I think and like the rest of the family possesses a firm belief in something shortly turning up. I have never met any family so suggestive of the Micawber philosophy. They seem to be able always mentally planning positions to turn up for them and their attitude is always that of preparing for a spring – but it must be society and not themselves, which must give the final impetus. Society is invited to step forward and redress their grievances. In the meantime they sit and wonder that such undoubtedly superior people shd. so long be left out in the cold. Harry is nearly 19 and is still at school. He is not bright I think altho' I think his father does. The whole family is quite offended if one suggests he might be getting his living instead of consuming the greater part of the family income. I can't say I have much patience with them all. I don't think Lilly liked Jessie very much. Jessie is, I am happy to say, an exceedingly practical work-a-day person and I think she told Lilly some rather rough truths apropos of their view of life. But it w'd take a long time to persuade Louisa and her daughter that it is not necessarily the mission of the Miss Joscelynes to make calls, pay rounds of visits and practise all the latest songs and dress charmingly. Jessie w'd say I exaggerate – but it is necessary to do so to make you understand the ludicrous aspect of the situation! I am afraid I am a dreadfully uncharitable fellow. But it is no good my telling you all the good things wh. on the other hand I see in people. All that you assume, and you are quite right as regards the Joscelynes.

Maude Lake is staying here. She is rather a contrast to Lilly Joscelyne who left the day before she came. She is so bright and restless and practical. She is, too, so charmed with her nephew. She can never have enough of him or ?talking and chattering to him . She is so proud to have a nephew – as proud as we are to have a son. The house is inundated with shoes and socks and sashes, head dresses and bibs which his 2 aunts send him.

I never seem to say anything to you about your own dear infants. What a happiness they must be to you – I am sure we know them quite well. We are longing to have a photograph of Dorothy whom we always speak of as "the perfect infant". She has been cutting her teeth, I expect, and if she made as much fuss as the Possum and Tots have done over it, I am afraid you will have had some bad nights. The dear old Possum is talking to you

now, I suppose, first getting up and asking endless questions –
kiss them both for me.

Give my best love to Oliver. Have you only got one
photograph of him – the one you sent me just before you were
married? I w'd like to have another of you c'd spare it. He is
frowning in the one we have – I sh'd like him minus the frown.
Goodbye my darling old pet sister. Ever your affectionate
brother, R.S.G.

December 11th 1877

My dearest Celia,

We have just returned from town rather tired having been to
an afternoon performance of the Opera Don Giovanni; my first
opera, so you can imagine what a treat it was to me, I enjoyed it
most thoroughly. At the same time I must confess that the
anticipatory exceeded the reality and I was disappointed not to
find myself completely carried out of myself. Instead of this at
no one time was I so engrossed to be unable to think about other
matters so I suppose I must meekly submit to Richard's
judgement viz that I have not enough soul for music. We did not
hear any of the stars today. I have at least acquired a taste for the
Opera for I have just induced Richard to promise to take me on
my birthday to hear Neillson* and then, if I am not completely
enraptured, I shall regard myself as hopelessly lost to the charms
of music.

Baby has been ill again with a bad cold but no bronchitis and
I am thankful to say he is better again now but looks very
delicate; he will be a year old on the 14th; we cannot let him
have a little party because unfortunately we do not know any

*   Christina Nilsson (1843-1921) the famous Swedish soprano.

children about here. He has already had one present, a lovely white cashmere frock braided with pale blue braid, this he will wear on Xmas Day with a little muslin pinafore and little blue kid shoes & white silk socks. He is such an old darling now and is devoted to his Mum,mum and Dad, dad.

Maude is staying with us now, she is so bright and such a chatterbox: she sends her best love to you and your little ones. Lily Joscelyne has been with us quite lately. She is painfully quiet but is a nice girl, although I found it rather hard to interest her in anything; she sings very well and practises most carefully every day. "The Message" she really sings charmingly and as you know it is a difficult song. I am afraid we could never become very good friends for she is not a baby lover; my dearest little man was quite a necessary toil in the house as far as Lily was concerned.

Richard has lately invested in a beautiful album in which he has mounted 2 dozen most exquisite photographs of Rome which Mrs. Cooper gave us; the mounting is a great success and they have all gone in quite smoothly, we find starch is the best thing for sticking photos.

We are as usual in domestic difficulties: our nurse turns out to be most untrustworthy. I should keep her as a general servant as she is a most excellent servant but this is impossible as she reports that Richard is so fond of her and spends hours in the kitchen begging her never to leave us and other ridiculous follies. This has amused us vastly, more especially as her idle gossip is credited by the Elite!! of Thornton Heath.

I have just had a black silk dress made, it is a plain princess with a robing of embroidery down the front which looks remarkably well; the material was a present from one of my Aunts.

1878

Rev. Henry Joscelyne

Louisa Joscelyne (née Gowlland)

Alice Joscelyne (?)

Lily Lake (?)

2 The Cedars,
Thornton Heath,
Surrey SE.

1 January 1878

My dearest Birdie,

Jessie and I wish you and Oliver and your dear babies a very happy and prosperous New Year.

We read with much pleasure your letter to Jessie which arrived just before Xmas day telling us that you were a grass widow and that Oliver had committed himself to the deep. I hope he returned well from his expedition.

How I sh'd enjoy to go out for a few days with him. I can imagine what yarns we sh'd tell each other. Your little daughter seems wonderfully to sustain her character of the best baby in the world – I cannot help casting angry looks at our offspring when I hear that she is even cutting her teeth with serene composure. As for my godson, I am sure I sh'd like him very much indeed. From your description of him, he is quite the boy after my own heart. Kiss them both for us.

Our boy is away at Gravesend. We came home today after spending a week there. The Tots is taking powders and cannot be allowed to return until the end of the week. The family was delighted with him. In the first 48 hours, however, he shrieked if Jessie or myself left him for a moment. He would not understand being left to the mercy of his aunts and the strange nurse. His own did not accompany us. But he soon became accustomed to the many new faces, showing a preference, however, for all the fair members of the family whose faces he patted with much complacency.

There was a great deal of rivalry and ill feeling between himself and his uncle aged 18 months. The uncle was discovered to pinch his nephew whenever he could be reached. The uncle would also rush across the nursery and push Tots over whenever he succeeded with much puffing and blowing in raising himself to his feet with the aid of a chair or somebody's dress. The Tots looked as if he was not without hopes that he would some day be in a position to punch his uncle's head – and indeed he has such a fine broad chest and such tough little arms and legs that I should not be afraid to back him to exact vengeance on his uncle in the course of a year or two. We quite cut out the uncle on Xmas day. The Tots was superb and sat through dessert helping himself to everything that came within his reach and dealing sturdy blows all round him with the largest spoon he could reach.

The Lakes were exceedingly genial and kind and seemed genuinely glad to have us with them. We dined one night at Wm. Lake's and another at the Grants at Aylesford. Today I spent at Malling with the Busbridges. They too were very glad to see me. Laura seems to be very happy and proud of her baby who seems to be a fine little girl.

Trot writes that she is much better. She had a week of bad sore throat just before Xmas which kept her in bed nearly a week and weakened her very much. I saw as much of the boys as I could – Harry, I hope, is coming here to spend a few days before his holidays end. Percy is going to spend some time with the Busbridges at Malling, and Arthur is staying with the Mackenzies in Harley Street until next week. Whitcombe has a sister staying with him. She is kind to the boys and appears to be less objectionable than the rest of the Whitcombe family.

Cont'd…

Annie, I am thankful to say, has found something to do. She is living at Windsor with a Mrs. Layard as companion to her daughter, a child of 13, who is very delicate in health and requires someone to be constantly with her. A nurse is with her in the evening and at night and Annie, as I understand it, is expected to walk with her and read to her and be generally useful during the day. The family consists of Captain & Mrs. Layard and one son. Mrs. Layard is sister to the Rector of Clewer, T.J. Larter, through whom Annie heard of the situation. It is just the sort of work she is able to do, I sh'd think; so I trust there is a good prospect of her remaining there.

We have been very much amused at your descriptions of the grandeur of Mrs. Living since her return from Europe. They are so precisely the counterpoint of what we were indulged in when she was here. Here she played off the grandeur of Sydney & Australia and her house at home against the narrow meanness of things to be seen here and the wretched lodgings she had to put up with in this uncivilized country. I liked Living very much; but I don't think I can feel the highest respect for a man who can sit and listen to his wife's follies unmoved. One w'd think it would be intolerable to any man of common honesty to hear without protest the sort of lying nonsense which he must be forever listening to.

Jessie is gone to bed with a cold and I must not sit up any longer or I shall invite her grave displeasure and be regaled with a certain lecture.

Wonder of wonders we received today an invitation to go to a party on the 8th at 34 Finsbury Square! We shall go and I must try to remember in my next letter to tell you about it.

Our best love to you & Oliver - kisses to the Babies – Ever your affec. Brother

R.S. Gowlland
Very many thanks for your proposal to give our boy a mug. It is exceedingly kind of you but I won't hear of your going in for such an extravagance. You must send him a keepsake one of

these days when someone is coming from Sydney. I can't tell you how dull we feel without our little Treasure. We are longing for his return. At Gravesend they call him the little Conductor because whenever he hears music or singing or even a bell ringing he proceeds to beat time! He has always been very fond of music from 3 months old! It was most amusing the other day. He was being soaped (preparatory to being dipped in his bath) a process he frankly objects to. He was bawling at the top of his voice when the dinner bell rang. He stopped crying instantly and gravely began to beat time. It was most ludicrous.

There is no other news. Goodbye and a happy 1878 to you all.

3 Jan 78

2, The Cedars,
Thornton Heath.
Surrey, S.E.

15 March 78

My dearest Birdie,

Many thanks for all the nice long letters I have rec'd. from you since I last wrote. There has been quite a fatality about my missing mails. It has quite put me out to think how long it is since I last wrote you a letter.

It is tremendously kind of Oliver to send Trot £10 and kinder still that you sh'd propose her coming to Australia. She will no doubt write to you about it. I sent her your letter and rec'd in the same mail £15 from Fred, £5 from himself and £10 for you. He recently sent me a draft of £5 for Trot. It will be a great relief to her to be able to stay on at Torquay as long as the cold weather lasts and we are just now entering upon our bitter

east winds. Today it is actually snowing! Trot is not so bad, I
hope, as you seem to think. Dr. Mackenzie told me that there
was no reason why with care she sh'd not make a perfect
recovery since as he said there was no organic disease. But that
she is very delicate and weak there can be no doubt. She is
naturally such an energetic woman that it is not a trifle which
could keep her tied to the house. I have good hope from the tone
of her letters that she is really much better. But it is an
idiosyncrasy of hers I think not to take the brightest view of her
own health. She has been in delicate health for so long that I
suspect she can hardly believe in getting quite strong.

At 9 o'clock on Monday (today is Friday) when we were
cosily sitting by the fire drinking our tea, a rat tat tat came to the
door and Annie walked in with all her bag and baggage. That
morning at Windsor her small charge was taken ill and at 5
o'clock the Dr. pronounced the sickness to be scarlet fever.
Annie at once packed up and came off to see us. I only hope and
trust that she hasn't brought us any infection for the fever must
be of a very virulent kind as the child died on Wednesday night!
So Annie is suddenly "without a home" as she expressed it much
to Jessie's disgust! She will stay with us until something turns up.
I asked her to write to you but she says you owe her shoals of
letters.

The only two episodes since I wrote to you are my making 2
speeches. One proposing the adoption of the report of the
Report at the General Meeting of the subscribers of the Throat
Hospital and another at a special meeting got up by certain
enemies of Marker given to injure his reputation. He was so
pleased with my remarks at the first meeting that he sent for me
to take up the question to be considered at the Board. I got all
the papers and correspondence to master the subject and I think
my speech was a great success. I would send you a copy of the
(report) containing it if I can get it. But when I applied to the

office for a spare copy it had been sold out. This is quite a new character isn't it? Dr. M. was quite profuse in his thanks, and I was exceedingly pleased to be able to be of some help to him. Certainly the result of my going into the question was to call attention to some important points in his favour which all the other speakers on his side quite overlooked.

Speaking to a lot of people has a curious effect on me. I get so excited that I can hardly speak at first, but when I am started, I rattle off with a vehemence and an earnestness which amuses me more than anything. You would think my life depended upon the issue! I am quite sure I wouldn't make a speech on any subject without my getting "worked up" in this way. I noticed that that manner was very telling. Certainly none of the speeches were applauded more than mine was.

I am always delighted with all you tell me about your sweet children. I am sure I couldn't...

Fragment of a letter written
about Easter 1878

...all that time and it hadn't even cut his skin. When he wakes in the morning the first half hours amusement consists in turning over his picture books. He kisses all his favourite animals. But he always shows a preference for a baby and if it is in a cradle he always puts his head down and says "bye bye."

Annie is here still and makes herself very useful to Jessie. She is an industrious needlewoman: the two sewing machines never seem to leave off. I think it must be like a factory. It is always a mystery to me that there can be so much needlework to be done for 3 people. Jessie is availing herself of Annie's help to replenish our linen stores I suppose! A has been up to London today to see Mr White. He comes up before the great festivals to dispense spiritual advice to some of his old flock. But Annie is going to write to you and will tell you all about him. The new Vicar of St Barnabas, Bagshawe seems to be a great deal more advanced than the Nuns approve of. Annie tells me that there is a commotion among them today that the palms for next Sunday are to be blessed with the help of Holy Water! I suppose this is another Roman Ceremony they have imported.

I must say the "Church has quite gone away from me. I suppose I am not so devout as I was or perhaps that w'd not be the case; but the fact is that I like a quiet service with as little Ritual as possible. It disturbs me, and in fact I never can get over the ludicrous aspect of it. It may be a strain of Protestantism which I have inherited but I cannot for the life of me enter into the feelings of people who attach such vast importance to small details. I cannot bring myself to believe that it matters one iota whether the priest stands in front of at the side of or behind the altar, whether candles are lighted or not, whether the priest is in a chasuble or in his shirt sleeves - and I am always regretting that for the sake of such matters good men sacrifice every day their chances of doing infinite good. I am quite prepared to find out some of these days that I was wrong but that is my personal feeling.

...I like very much the Parson of the church where I sing in the choir. The Vicar recently lost his wife and the congregation have decided to begin a permanent church as a memorial to her. The present church is a temporary iron one. The parish has only just been created: it is a District of Norwood and Croydon. I am sorry that it is a little too far off for Jessie to walk there very often.

I had a very nice letter from Fred two days ago. He tells me that he had seen you at Sydney just before he wrote. He says that he has just sold his "Buggy" (what a barbarous word that is, worse than Wagga Wagga!) and horse and is going in for

John Lake (Jessie's grandfather)

Richard (?)

Jack (?)

economy. He also tells me of the birth of his daughter on the 10th of Feb. He complains of having a cough very often. I am afraid he is not constitutionally stronger than the rest of us.

...other day but I was not there. He had just come back from ?Inalvarne.

Jessie sends her best love to you all. My love to Oliver and kisses to the dear children. Ever your very affectionate

R.S.G.

I w'd never venture to send such an ill-written letter to anyone but you. But I think you w'd make out an even worse griffonnage from me. I send you some photos of Oxford by this mail. They are small but they are the best I could get here. I strongly recommend you to have them framed two to a frame with a margin.

I have a distinct idea of you house and garden...your house. I am always longing forward to getting the photographs of...

2, The Cedars, Thornton
Heath, SE
11 April 78

My dearest Birdie,

Your letter to Jessie enclosing a letter for Trot reached us some time ago. We were delighted to hear good news of you all and to read your charming accounts of your babies. So many things you say apply to our Tots. He likes nothing better than a spoon. He will walk about all day with one in his hand and the bigger the better he likes it. I expect he will take one to church with him when he goes. He surprises me by saying little new words every day almost. But he has been ill with the mumps since I wrote to you last. He was very ill for three or four days and he and we got very little sleep. At the best of times I don't think Jessie gets enough sleep for the Boy wakes at half past five and has no rest after that. We unfortunately have got into the habit of going to bed late – the result of a visitor (Annie) in the house – we always find that makes us later. There is so much more packing up before we can get off – Jessie is looking very seedy just now and is not so well as she ought to be. We have just settled down again in the matter of domestics. We have two rough creatures who as anyone… (? by honest teaching). But they seem to require an immense amount of looking after and that is Jessie's business. She never appears to get …

.rocks to view before me that I could draw them at the moment. Of course the photographs will dispel my illusion. But most often I like to stand in your garden and look across the bay and see the waves gently lapping the rocks and your boats riding at anchorage. I won't say that I always quit the spot without regretting that I have…initially what…(?seeming) always the better I…

The Cedars,
Thornton Heath,
Surrey S.E.

1 August 78

My dearest Birdie,

Annie has written you a very long letter and Jessie another which, I enclose herewith and I only hope the postage stamps will carry 'em.

I am ashamed not to have written to you for such a long time. I am sensible of being a brute. It must be 6 weeks ago since my last letter to you. It so happened I got into a bad draught when the mail was on the eve of departure – caught a bad cold and was laid up for a week or more at home quite without courage to do anything beyond the study of the manners of the Micawber family as set forth in David Copperfield. I don't know what I sh'd do without the Micawbers when my wife and my offspring fail to raise or interest me but Mr and Mrs Wilkins and the twins come to my rescue (the twins you will remember because one or other of them (was) always taking refreshment!!)

To begin at my latest occupation – yesterday I went to Epsom to see the prizes given away by Sir James Paget. Percy did not get one but Willie did. Willie is a quiet delicate little boy. Percy however carried off what most boys prize beyond books the bat for the highest average score made by any boy during the term. He was here just now displaying it to me with a silver shield and inscription upon it. Sir James Paget, a nice old man, made an excellent speech. Trot was well to the fore with Arthur in a white sailor suit looking the greatest swell on the premises and the two eldest sons of Dr. Mackenzie boys of 10 and 12 who had come down to see the fun. It seemed rather hard that Percy had no prizes to take – I shouldn't wonder if the cricket had something to do with it! It is rather unfortunate that he has just failed for the second time in the Preliminary Scientific Examination at the University of London. He won't be able to go in for that again for another year which is a great drawback. This is his last term at school – I don't know what his father's programme is for him. At any rate he has given him an excellent groundwork for more practical knowledge.

I thought by this time I sh'd have been able to tell you something of our new fils or fille. But it is not yet to be. I am afraid now we shall be completely cheated out of any holiday this year - for it will hardly be worth going away late in September and in the best event we can hardly get away in the

early part of the month. Annie has been here for months and
months awaiting this event and has made herself very useful.
She is a quiet old thing whom after a time one does not notice in
the house at all. Louisa now and Trot are always talking and
prevent one's reading which irritates me in the long run. But
Annie's silence is a great virtue and advantage. Trot is
surprisingly well and strong I think. She can certainly do a great
deal more than either Jessie or Annie can do in the best of times.
Yesterday after the speeches at Epsom we had only 20 minutes to
walk 1 mile (?very) quickly to the station. The day was hot the
road dusty but Trot did it easily. She had come up from
Gravesend that morning (having only the previous day returned
from staying with the Hewitts at the Isle of Wight) went to
Harley Street thence to Waterloo and Epsom, walked 1 ¼ miles
to the college and as I said walked back. I think we may consider
her invalid period over.

Of our own amusements and proceedings I can tell you
nothing since we never move and we never proceed. The Boy is
our joy and pride and only amusement. We note his little pranks
and advances in intelligence with the keenest interest and
pleasure. He is a pale little fellow and I often think that other
people would probably hold up their hands in amazement at our
giving up so much time and thought to such an insignificant
little mite. He talks wonderfully for his age - can say all sorts of
things now and practically understands all that he is told. His
great weakness is dabbling in water with soap and sweeping the
carpets and the garden path with my hand brush. He also is very
fond of digging with any little stick and trowel he can find. He
delights chiefly in Jessie and my society but he is also much
attached to "Anna" who has him to sleep in her room. I am happy
to say he sleeps very well now. He usually looks out for my
return home in the evening and will run down the road to meet
me with his two little hands up and on his face a broad grin of

delight. As soon as he reaches me however he becomes engrossed in something else – a stone or a weed or a dog passing and usually declines to go back with me but expresses a desire to continue his promenade with me if possible but alone if I decline to accompany him. He inherits his mother's dislike of food: it is seldom he eats what would appear to be necessary for him.

Of Louisa we hear nothing except that all her children are at home for the holidays and that they go out to a great many parties.

I have found a cricket club and play occasionally but it is needless to say I never make long scores or otherwise distinguish myself. I still sing in my Choir at Norwood but I am afraid I shall have to give it up. It is conducted so badly and there is such a provoking waste of time at practices. Jessie always laughs when I talk of giving things up. She is of the opinion that I tire of everything after a short time - I am afraid I don't possess the sticking power of some people – of people especially I find this the case. I wear them out - very quickly. But I remember I told you all this ever so often before. There is nothing like having a critical wife at one's elbow to lay out one's own weaknesses. Well, Goodbye, I hope you and Oliver and the bairns are quite well. I think I shall call the new infant if a boy Oliver. I have a great weakness for the first Protector and then it is your name. Love to Oliver and kisses to the Bairns. Ever yr. afft. R.S.G.

Jessie has written her letter upon such very thick paper. I'm tremulous of sending it under a fortune for postage. She must write to you again soon. I (? believe that the most part of the) letter was about "Ebbard" as he calls himself and contained a drawing by him. Annie (?reserves) her letter to you until there is some important news to communicate. What do you think of the

Peace, in Australia? There is a great deal of throwing up of caps here.[*]

2, The Cedars,
Thornton Heath,
Surrey S.E.

15 August 78

My dearest Birdie,

Thanks for your two letters, one en miniature enclosing a letter for Trot the other a long account of your friends the Moriartys, the Nivisons and the Bennetts. I have not yet seen Mrs. Bennett. She is at Cheltenham but comes up to Town next week when I will call upon her. Jessie remarks with regret that your letter contains no mention whatever of your infants and since you abused me a long time ago for giving my impression of Mrs.Living so now I beg to administer a reprimand to you for devoting the whole of your letter to those excellent people whose acquaintance I am to make. Jessie remarks that she thinks you are becoming a "woman of the world". I don't quite know what she means by that; perhaps it will convey some sense to you but as Jessie said it regretfully I assume she prefers people who are not of this world. This comes I suppose of being not of this world as we do in Thornton Heath.

The long expected event came off on Thursday the last 8th Inst. Jessie came down to breakfast that morning feeling just the thing. I went off to my office as usual but came back at 12 feeling anxious about my little wife. I found the little daughter

---

* The Congress of Berlin in which Bismark mediated an elaborate compromise between the Russian and Austrian interests in the Balkans and probably averted a European war. Britain got Cyprus as part of the deal.

had arrived an hour after I left home. Jessie has made good progress. She is only troubled a good deal with neuralgia. She is told to eat and drink quantities and it is fortunate that her appetite is better than when she is up and about. The little girl is a nice baby with quite a woman's face and a peculiarly soft sweet little mouth.

While I think of it will you please send a drawing of the stocking you want. It is not enough to have an old one. Send measurements on a drawing of the leg and I will put it in the hands of my stocking maker. The measurement from the heel round the instep sh'd be given. I am afraid, however, that the heat of the tropics will be likely to injure the elastic. If it does not there is no reason why the stockings sh'd not be sent by post. We shall see. I will not forget the card case which you want. I am glad the Oxford photographs reached you safely. I will try again to get one of the Chapel of Exeter.

I am glad to hear that Aleck's appointment to the new post of Parliamentary Draughtsman had been made. I wish he could exchange with some one here who wants a change of air. What a jolly little Colony we would make at some quiet suburban village. I am sure you would be delighted with my dear old Tots. He grows more charming every day and learns new tricks. It is beautiful to see him bow when he wishes anyone good morning. He has never been so delighted at anything as the new baby. He rolls about with laughter when he sees her and screams till she is put in his arms and he can put his little head against the other very much smaller head and coo himself with rapture!!!

Of Trot and Louisa I can tell you no news. They are both as far as we know quite well together with their Gefolge*. Mary Joscelyne spent a few hours with us on the way to school at Berlin. She appears to be a very sensible pleasant girl and is

---

*   attendants

Countess Elizabeth of Austria

Emperor of Austria

decidedly pretty. Best love to Oliver and kisses to Marcius and Dorothy. I am going to make you the Godmother to my girl. She is to be called Katherine Mary. I am going to ask the Sister Superior to be the other Godmother. Ever yr. afft. R.S.G.

Brighton
8 Oct. 78.

My dearest Birdie,

I wrote to Oliver by the last mail about the books. I meant to have sent a separate letter to you but somehow didn't. This will go by the Frisco mail which leaves London on Thursday. I enclose a receipt which Oliver will have to present to get a second parcel of books which I sent by the next outgoing P & O mail. The parcel contains Sir James (? Fitzstephen's)Bill for the reform of the Criminal Code and the Report of the Royal Commission on Friendly Societies. Also the cards you ordered and four Photographs of Exeter Coll: Chapel – the best and largest I could find in London.

We came down here a fortnight ago at least Jessie and the babies did – I followed a fortnight later. We have had very good weather so far; it has been wonderfully warm for the time of the year so that the infants have been able to spend the whole day on the beach. We found very fair lodgings close to the sea where, barring the fleas which eat-up poor old Peeps, we are very comfortable. Jessie is remarkably well and her little daughter is a model. She sleeps the whole night and when she wakes patiently waits till it is convenient to give her refreshment. Her behaviour reminds one of what you told us of Dorothy at the same age. We used to be filled with wonder and envy at your accounts of her goodness. Now our little one is just as good. It is a great blessing. I don't know what would have become of us if we had had another edition of the Peeps. He is very little trouble now, however, provided that care be taken to remove from view whatever suggests certain wants. If a pen or paper or a bottle of ink or pencil is visible he will not rest until he can engage someone to draw a "gee-gee". He gravely overlooks the performance as it is proceeding and immediately corrects any omissions – "Tail too" " Bip too" "Man too" are his remarks if any of these are left out. He is a quaint little man – very old fashioned I sh'd say. He will amuse himself quite alone for a long time. On the beach and sand with a shovel and bucket we have not yet exhausted his powers of amusing himself. He makes himself thoroughly wet and dirty it is needless to say. Jessie couldn't get to church the Sunday before I came down without taking the Peeps too. Accordingly they went up to St. Paul's. He behaved very well for a time but just before the beginning of the service as he was getting fidgety Jessie gave him her prayer book. This he at once put on the top of his head, as he had seen men in the streets carry their baskets, and shouted at the top of his voice and in clear unmistakeable tone three or four times "Any old rags or bones". Once set off there was no stopping him. He had to be carried forthwith out of the church.

We have just had bad news of Annie. Sister wrote to tell me that she had been to see the Physician who had been prescribing for Annie for some time past. She had been suffering violent pain from indigestion during her stay with us but the pain grew worse after she went to Pimlico and she went to consult a Physician. His remedies did not appear to improve matters much and to her symptoms were added a great deal of oppression in the region of the heart. The Physician told Sister that her heart was seriously affected and that she must take great care of herself. She is come down to Preston to stay with the Goulds and I am just going over to see her. If you should be writing to her you should be careful not to mention that you have heard she has disease of the heart. The Doctors say nothing does people more harm suffering from it than to know that they have it. They are perpetually worrying about it and it is just worry which aggravates the disease. Trot was to have taken Annie to see Dr. Mackenzie on Monday and I hope to hear from her that Mackenzie thinks the other Dr. has exaggerated the matter. In any case it is very serious. I have just heard from Trot. Mackenzie unfortunately confirms the other Dr.'s opinion. Poor dear old Annie. I am exceedingly sorry. She will come and live with us now. She is quite unfit for any work at present. Either rest and great care may so far restore her health as to remove the actual pain from which she has been suffering – but the disease itself I am afraid is incurable. I saw her yesterday at Preston. She was still suffering from want of sleep. She will come here in a day or two.

I went to see the Nivisons before leaving Town. I was surprised to find that they had been everywhere and seen everything and were quite used up. They had been 5 weeks in London. My advice to Australians (?thinking of) taking a voyage to England is "Don't". Sydney they all tell me is so much finer in every respect than anything we have here that it is an obvious waste of money to leave Australia. Miss Nivison is no exception. The shops, the streets and buildings, the hotels, the private houses, the Society are all superior at Sydney. I remained about two hours with them and this was the only burden of their song! One finds it rather monotonous. It appears to be the only topic of conversation the Australians I have met take any interest in. I am afraid it is a cardinal colonial defect. It's American swagger in its infancy. Miss Nivison also tells me that everything is infinitely cheaper in Sydney from jewellery to shoelaces. She is much impressed by the want of civility of people in English shops. In this matter especially Sydney again is far ahead of us.

Adieu. Best love to Oliver and kisses to the dear children. Many thanks for the photographs – I was charmed with them and so is everyone who sees them. The superiority of the Sydney infant I sh'd be quite prepared to admit! Ever your afft. R.S.G.

The Moriartys haven't turned up yet.

                                        Brighton
                                        Oct. 8 1878

My dearest Celia,

You must be thinking very badly of me, it is such an age since you have heard from me. I wrote you a long letter a few days before the birth of our dear wee daughter, but Richard, finding that his letter was an improved version of mine, and that mine would make it overweight, did not send it. It is curious that we should both have a son first and then a daughter; although we should have, or fancied we should have, been better pleased had little Katherine Mary been a 2nd son.

We are so proud of the little pair and could not possibly love our little girlie more than we do, she is a perfect little thing and gives us no trouble at all; not nearly as much as the old Peeps who is getting so sharp and adventurous that he requires constant attendance; he is a most original little man and always causes quite an excitement wherever he goes; he talks beautifully and can even deliver messages most satisfactorily.

I know you will be glad to hear I am feeling and looking stronger than I have done for a very long time, in fact everyone is astonished at my improved appearance; little baby too depends upon me entirely for sustenance and her little fat cheeks and firm hands betoken that she fares very well.

We have been adventurous enough to attempt Brighton again this year and we are now enjoying the most charming

weather, it is so warm that we can sit on the beach all day. I quite
dread going home again for it was very cold at Thornton Heath
when we left, so our little trip will make our winter delightfully
short.

I find I have quite as much as I can manage with the two
babies, and only a young nurse girl: if the wee darling had been
as delicate as the Peeps was I don't know what I should have
done. We have nice lodgings and contrive to be out nearly all
day.

Richard spent a week of his leave at Fewcott and enjoyed his
visit very much indeed; he always finds out the warm corner of
everyone's heart and is a favourite wherever ho goes. I feel I can
never be thankful enough for such a dear husband and my
darling babies - Louisa is continually laughing when Richard is
with her and I think he makes her feel ten years younger.

You will be sorry to hear that poor Annie has been very far
from well lately and still more sorry and distressed to hear that
the doctors pronounced her to be in an extremely delicate state.
She has been to Dr. Mackenzie and another good doctor and
they both say her heart is much affected. She is not to know
herself; they have told her it is weak only, so you must be careful
in writing to her. We hope to take us back with us to Thornton
Heath to live with us, and she is such a dear good-tempered
creature that it is a real pleasure and a privilege to be able to offer
her a home and she is so devoted to Richard and the babies that I
hope she will be happy with us. She is now staying at Preston
with some friends of hers, the Goulds, so she is close to us and
will accompany us home.

Richard says he has only room for one sheet from me so I
must say goodbye and goodnight; like you it is generally
bedtime when I write my letters. I do not know when to expect
news of you but, dear Celia, you have my warmest sympathy and

very best wishes for you and those dear darlings of yours. Very best love to you all, your loving sister, Jessie K.Gowlland.

The Cedars, Thornton
Heath, Surrey
24 Oct. 78

My dearest Birdie,

We have just got back from Brighton. We had wonderful weather there and sunny almost every day. I was able to bathe up to the 18th of the month. Jessie and both babies are much better for the change – Jessie has never been better and the new girl is as fat and cheerful as possible. I had them all photographed at Brighton and (I'll) send you copies. The boy is the failure. He was taken 6 times, but he always moved and when he didn't move as in the copy he frowned horridly so that everyone who sees the Photograph exclaims with horror that it is a shame and a scandal that he should be handed down to prosperity so ill-looking. It is quite clear that he must be either extremely interesting-looking or else pretty for we find everyone raves about him. Now you are not going to (?wince) over the portrait less it is not a good one.

Annie we left at Preston where she proposes to spend a couple of weeks more with the Goulds. She seems a trifle better. Her looks are not much improved however but she admits her heart is less troublesome and that she gets more sleep – but the violent indigestion cannot be got rid of although she has taken a variety of remedies to cure it. She will come to us when she leaves the Goulds. The Sisters are anxious that she should go back to them but it won't do. They don't the least spare an invalid I notice – or rather they don't admit invalidishness for any length of time. Poor old Hukie's lethargy for some time past is now well accounted for. It appears her heart must have been affected for a long time. I wonder if we all carry about with us the inherited weak heart. You know it is what killed our mother. It is curious that Annie sh'd be suffering acutely at her age from both the diseases which were fatal to our father and mother. He you know really died of indigestion.

Percy Whitcombe called to see me yesterday. You will have heard of his gaining the 1st. Scholarship at St. Mary's Hospital. Trot is as happy as a Queen about it. It is most creditable to Percy. He had only good men against him it seems. It is a curious change of life for him from his quiet of school to be working all day long in the heart of London with exciting work too. The day he called to see me he had been whittling away at dissecting a gentleman's leg all morning, assisting at an operation in the afternoon and (?that is not to) mention lectures. Louisa has just taken her third boy Arthur to a school at Eastbourne. He is in a choir there and is therefore educated at a very low figure at a good school in the town. Nothing further has turned up for Harry who is at home working for the Hertford Scholarship at Oxford. The examination is to be held early next month. If he doesn't get it I expect he will go to Ceylon coffee planting. He knows some people who have friends there who recommend him to go. I suppose there is no opening for him in Australia?

The Moriartys haven't turned up at my office during my absence. I have had to give up Mrs. Bennett since I can't follow her to Cheltenham. The Nivisons I must look up again. When I saw them last they were expecting to go to Brighton but they didn't turn up there. Do you know that your Australians are extremely heavy people!!! They have talk of nothing but Sydney! They appear to me to be much more foreign than either Germans or Frenchmen are to us here – and have no sympathy with our doings at all and treat us always with a good-natured contempt I notice – even the best of them such as these Nivisons

do it. Living didn't because he was (an) Englishman but his wife did to an insufferable degree. Goodbye and best love to Oliver. How thankful I am that he is an Englishman! Best love from Jessie to you and kisses to the babies. Ever yr. aff. R.S.G.

So you have a train all the way to Wagga Wagga now I see – you will be deserting your Lord and master and your off spring to go and spoon with Fred!!!! He sends me a newspaper from time to time just to remind me that he still exists.

                                        Thornton Heath SE
                                        18 Nov 78 Monday

My dearest Birdie,

I have just received the joyful news of the birth of your second little daughter. Jessie and I are delighted to hear that you and the baby were so well when Oliver wrote. Many thanks to him for his letter. I received it that day seven weeks and the San Frisco mail, which he mentioned as having arrived while he wrote and as having been put in quarantine, contained a letter I expect telling you of the birth of our little daughter who was born on the 8th of August. There is just seven weeks and three days between the cousins – a "Mail" between us and when we write to tell you of our Katherine Mary's tricks, the letter will reach you just when your baby has attained the same age. Well, there is not much to relate of the young person here. Happy is the country and also the baby that has no history. More specially happy in room (NB what a gorgeous room, how I envy you it, a bedroom can't be too big. We have no room 19 x 30 x 22 so that this is perhaps not so wonderful as would at first sight appear). She seems to know the Peeps and is specially cheerful and laughing when he deigns to play with her. He is genuinely fond of her and kisses her with effusion whenever he is permitted to

fondle her. It is charming to see them together. I sent you her
photograph last mail so you will be able to see what she is like.
Her hair, which was thick when she was born, came off and is
now growing again. Her eyes, which are fine, are blue.

Annie is settled here now for the winter. She is decidedly
better but then Dr. Mackenzie insists on her coming to him
every fortnight. He evidently thinks she requires watching. Her
heart is much quieter but she still has a bad hour or so at night. It
takes the form of shivering fits. She has then to take hot brandy
and water – cold is no good. So she sleeps with a spirit lamp
beside her so as to be prepared. We never let her go upstairs
more than once or twice a day. So she sits and knits or works all
day long; she is very quiet and seems to be thoroughly happy
here. She is immensely fond of the babies and cannot see enough
of them. The old Peeps generally goes up to play in her bedroom
while she is dressing in the morning.

We had bad news today from Fewcott. Louisa is laid up.
They were afraid she was really very seriously ill. The Doctor
had to be summoned in the middle of the night. Lilly, too, is in
bed. Have you heard that a living has been offered to them at
last; Fingest-cum-Ibstone 6 miles N. of Henley on Thames.
Merton College gave it to them. They go there in the spring.
There is a fine house and £300 a year but for the present the old
Rector takes a third of that enormous income. When he dies they
will have the whole sum. There are two churches situated two
miles apart. Ir will therefore be absolutely necessary to keep a
pony or a curate. The former being the cheaper and more
generally useful animal will be preferred, I expect.

I can't help agreeing in what you say about the
unsatisfactoriness of letter-writing as an only means of
communication. There is necessarily something forced about it.
But so there is often about conversation. The advantage of talk is
that it suggests topics and is less solemn than writing. It is far

easier to keep up a warm interchange of thought with people only received a day's post from one. In writing to Australia one is rather oppressed by the feeling that one's words are going to exist for two whole months. One necessarily approaches the operation with some gravity. But as you say, "Quoi faire" – we must make the best of it. After all it is astonishing how little pleasant talk one ever gets with anyone. The element of nonsense and badinage is necessarily eliminated from letters, which is to be lamented – one can't laugh much.

I don't believe one could ever get to form even a decently correct opinion of anyone by post. I always feel rather on stilts with a pen in my hand (women don't feel this as much as men but they are not free from it). Jessie, for instance, is much more stilted in letters than in reality, and this quite unconsciously for she is the most natural soul alive with not the tiniest grain of humbug in her composition. I don't know a single person so free from it. So one must conclude that it is a natural and unavoidable infirmity this unreality in letter writing. Your letters are far the best and most natural that I ever read, so consider yourself quite excluded from the view of these sweeping assertions.

Australia will always remain a puzzle to me. You say fruit is dear and less good than in England. Every single Australian I have seen grumbles and growls at the scarcity and nastiness of everything here, fruit included. I shall tell them all in future that distance lends enchantment to the view.

Trot sent me to read a long letter she had received from ?Jager Nichols. He writes very well. Gave a very good description of Sydney and your house and neighbourhood. Most of the letter was devoted to the praise of Jennie who appears to have quite won his heart, which I didn't consider any great certificate to the soundness of his judgement. Of course, Jennie's coming to England is a mere joke,. Pray explain to her, if the project is seriously entertained, that I cannot even offer her a bed if she turned up here. As to helping her with money that would be quite out of the question in as much as I simply haven't enough to do more than pay my own bills. She would be the most miserable of creatures here. The monotony of the sort of life we lead, not a soul coming to the house for months at a time, w'd drive her to despair. It is most distressing to hear that her boys are so unruly. Is there no brother of hers who would at any rate break the pipes which you mention as being indispensable to their existence? Why doesn't she settle at Wagga and let Fred see what he could do with them. I don't know anything of the Wellmans but what you have seen and heard of the Lords convinces me that I entirely agree with Oliver in his appreciation of them.

Both our infants sleep in our room. The cradle is on Jessie's side and the cot on mine. The baby doesn't wake at night. The boy rouses at about half past three pretty regularly and is taken in to the "big bed". I had a long fight with him the other night to see if he couldn't be broken of this bad habit. He screamed and sobbed for half an hour lying quite still in his cot – it was too distressing – to all my soothing talk he only said between his sobs over and over again "please Faver dear take me over". He won at last of course. I suppose we shall have another battle royal again very shortly. I am told it is very weak to give way: having a real baby makes me regard the Peeps as quite amenable to reason. But of course he is quite a baby, only a year and 11 months now. We are going to have a flare up on his 2nd birthday – a Christmas tree and 3 infants (all we know) to tea! We were talking just now of your picnic on Marcius's second birthday – I hope the Peeps will be more amiable – but all his guests will be just his own age about. He is always delighted to have children to play with. He is a little jealous of the baby. He often says "Take it away" when he wants to sit in his old place on his 'mummy's' lap. He is extremely sharp – passing a gate where Jessie had called with him some days before, he stopped and said "wants to see the Ady (Lady)".

Goodbye my dearest Birdie – our best love to Oliver and kisses to the babies. Ever yr. afft. RSG

1879

2 The Cedars, Thornton
Heath.
2 January 1879

My dearest Birdie,

I wish you and Oliver and your dear Chicks a very happy
New Year.

How is Katherine behaving? Our Kate kept remarkably well
until Christmas day when Jessie went skating all the afternoon
and enjoyed herself so much that the excitement affected the
infants' refreshment and she has since been ailing and taking
powders. She keeps up her spirits however and declines
altogether to be considered an invalid. She laughs and takes a
great deal of notice. She evidently knows her mammy and is said
to weep when she leaves the house, but of this latter detail I have
my doubts. She is a sweet little being, possessing an exceedingly
placid temper. She will submit to all kinds of neglect without
murmuring. I am very fond of her indeed – perhaps the more
because she is so much like you. It must be so, for everyone who
knows you both remarks it. She recalls to me what you were as a
little girl in pinafores most especially, but she also has your later
look. She still sleeps almost all the night, I am glad to say.

The dear old Peeps sleeps on my side in his cot; about seven
every morning he shouts for me. I generally find that before he
has succeeded in waking me (he) has poised himself on the rail
of the cot in such a position that he can neither move backwards
or forwards his head being out and his legs in. He is always
being most charming. We keep up our romps from 5 to 6 and
indeed his father is so fond of him that after his bath he generally
comes down to the dining room to witness the eating of
pudding and to be made much of. Then he lights my pipe and
sits on my knee until the inexorable nurse arrives: she is always
greeted with howls. "No I don't "ike it" is often repeated on the

stairs and occasionally he bites and pulls the young person's hair down. For offences of this magnitude, however, I understand he is whipped. He is always very penitent Jessie says and bears no malice. We have got this charming book of songs given to us, and these I sing to him a good deal. He is always wrapped in delight and however long the songs are he wishes for more.

I intended to write a long letter but have got instructions to go over to the Customs House which is at the other end of old London and I must be off without delay as it is late in the afternoon.

Annie is much better. She is staying in London for a week with the Sisters. The Sister Superior is the Godmother to our Kate as you know. She is always sending the infants things. She is more especially in love with the Peeps who comes up to see her occasionally with Jessie. There seems to be no prospect of Annie's ever being well enough to do anything again, so that we look upon her as a permanent inmate of our house. She sits knitting or writing all day long in the same chair. Jessie tells me that she never moves from morning to night. Trot and the boys have been spending Xmas with the Hewitts and have enjoyed themselves very much. We had a very happy Christmas at the Cedars and a splendid afternoon skating. Jessie got on very well. Louisa still continues poorly and weak. Mary leaves Berlin this week and is going to school at the Queens College. Harry Joscelyne still unoccupied. I understand they are about to spend about £100 in doing up their new home in Ibstone. They move in March.

Goodbye, I must be off. My love and best wishes for the New Year to you both and kisses for the bairns. Yours Aff. R.S.G.

We are going to a party at Peter Gowlland's on the 15th. Private theatricals.

April 1879.

Jessie begs me to tell you that Katherine Mary cut her first tooth on the 22nd of March "also" as the Germans say at the age of seven months and 14 days. The first tooth looks so queer I always think. There is a solitary appearance about it and a want of proper balance. The 2nd tooth came on the 8th inst. at exactly 8 months. Now how about your baby's tooth? We shall feel hurt and humiliated if you have more teeth than we have!! I could rave to you for six sheets about the virtues and beauty of Katherine Mary, but enough of that. She can roll herself into any position she desires to occupy on the floor with astonishing rapidity. She is more fond of the cat than of either of her parents. Next to the cat she loves the boy. She makes furious efforts to be attractive to him and to keep him at her side – but she too (insistently) demonstrates her affection by pulling his hair to render him very anxious to play with her. She continues to be the best baby on record – sleeps all night and is good all day. The dear old Boy who is still as charming and loveable as ever, has been banished from our room to the Night nursery where he sleeps much better for if he wakes up there in the night his nurse gets him off again quickly whereas with me he always insisted on sitting up and holding a long conversation.

I find I haven't time to write any more – a man has been in, an old neighbour at Thornton Heath, and has taken up the half hour I meant to write to you in.

Goodbye. My best love to Oliver and kisses to the bairns. I trust they are well and the nurse crisis is overpast.

Ever yr. aft. R.S.G.

9 May 79.

My dearest Birdie,

What a charming boy yours must be and how I would like
him to stay with me. I think he is a splendid fellow and I am glad
you have resolved it is no good trying to thrash him into
submission. I sometimes think that I am much more likely to see
him than to see you again. For I suppose if he sh'd develop any
striking talent you will want to send him over here to try his
hand against the young prodigies at our schools and universities.
It seems to me always uncommonly hard that we are never to see
you – for that is what it amounts to. I always regard with
wonderful calmness any rumours of the impending dissolution
of this branch of H.M. Service (not that there is any at the
present moment) because it would secure me the pleasure of
seeing you again. That is the only chance now – that the P.W.D.
sh'd dispense with my services.

There is no news whatever. Annie I see was writing to you all
yesterday evening and has probably remembered all the
incidents better than I could. It is a great bore to hate letter
writing as much as I do. In other words it is a great bore to have
no imagination – but added to that it wearies me to see my bad
writing! The mechanical effort of writing is a nuisance – some
people even like that. Annie must I am sure for she always had a
prim self-satisfied expression on her face when she is writing as
if she were engaged in something eminently virtuous. She
always writes in such a stilted manner too, quite different from
her talk. I suppose the self-complacency in that case arises from
a sense of turning out a very fine composition!

Louisa spent an evening with us recently. She is as merry as
ever although she tells you she is crushed at the thought of all
the bills they owe and cannot pay. But that is not the fact. This
morning for instance she wrote to me that they had just got in

the bill for doing up the house £120 and a lot of others she mentioned: they have no prospect of paying any of them and she was depressed she said about it - but - she added at the end of her letter, this is so characteristic that I send it to you - " but what vexes and troubles me most of all is that I can't match the cord for my new drawing room curtains which I bought when I was in London."

Jessie and the babies have been spending a week at Gravesend. I have escaped going down happily on one pretext or another. I cannot stand the people at all. However they seem to be very civil to Jessie and the infants. The dear old Peeps seems to be homesick however; I shall be extremely glad to have him back again.

We still haven't found a house. I don't know what will be done. I cannot find any house sufficiently good for the outside rent we can pay or price we could pay in which I can think we sh'd care to spend all our days.

I will send out y'r chairs as soon as I hear when the Paramatta is about to start. I will try and find out but I am not sure I shall succeed.

My best love to Oliver and kisses to the dear chicks.

Ever y'r loving R.S.G.

11 Whitehall Place.
4 August 1879

My dearest Birdie,

Many thanks for your letter of the 10th May. We were most grieved to hear that you had had so much illness in the house. I am afraid your boy must be growing too fast. Tonsillitis does not seem to be well known here at any rate. I suppose it arises from cold getting on a weak constitution. I had something very like what you describe when I was 15. I never got well till my tonsils had been removed. I have had hardly any trouble with my throat since that operation, which however I could not recommend anyone to submit to unless performed by an operating surgeon and under anaesthetic.

However I trust Marcius will have recovered without any such violent remedies. It is most painful to have children ill. If the least thing ails either of my pets I am quite ill too with anxiety – just as if a cloud were always hanging over me. Happily we have small cause for anxiety. The little one underwent a slight crisis when her food was recently changed from condensed milk to cow's milk – she became quite weak and an invalid in 24 hours from sickness. But she soon picked up again and is very strong now. She is apparently bright and intelligent – is devoted to her mother and will only "fly to" anyone else when there is a prospect of going for a walk for which she has a passion if for anything at all. The dear Peeps too is quite well. He and I are greater friends than ever and I never can have enough of his society. We are always romping when I am at home and he is not in bed. He comes in to spoon in my bed in the morning after he has had his bath. He is most easily amused. At present we are engaged in pursuing an imaginary mouse which is extracted from my neck and I from his with roars of laughter!! Is this one of your favourites – we have rather checked his learning things. He became too knowing and thought too much. Picture books are his delight when he is too tired to romp. He knows animals and fishes and birds now. I think he mixes them purposely sometimes when he is being shown off – so that his wisdom suffers from his insisting on calling a hippopotamus a peacock on field days.

Many thanks to you both for the £10 which I duly received. As I said before you have no business to send it – but it nevertheless is most acceptable and will be most useful. We certainly are beginning to find it difficult to make both ends meet. All the same we are going to take a holiday again this year in our old lodgings at Brighton. I am going the first 10 days of my leave to make a walking tour with a Mr Fox whom you have heard of from us. We propose to go along the N coast of Devonshire and Cornwall starting on the 25th Inst. I hope it won't be very hot weather. We are going to carry knapsacks. Jessie will be during that time at Brighton where I shall join her after I return from the west.

Annie is gone to Ibstone to the Joscelynes; she does not appear to be so well there as with us. She never sleeps well away from us and appears to be quite homesick whenever she is long absent.

Alice Joscelyne aged 15 is staying with us for 3 weeks. A quiet child rather heavy but persevering and slow at learning. I am teaching her French in the evening. I thought I sh'd have had a fit when I heard her pronunciation. All she knows she has learnt from her father and I can answer for it that his Reverence w'd not make himself understood over the water.

There is no further news of any interest to you. Singularly little happens to disturb the even tenor of our way. And so it is best of course for we are then as happy as the days are long.

I am in charge here at the present moment and am deluged with work so that I have had to write to you in the intervals of it at snatches.

My best love to Oliver and kisses to the chicks. I trust when this reaches you they will be all well and indeed that they were so long since.

Ever y'r afft R.S.G

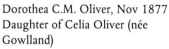

Edward Lake Gowlland, Richard and
Jessie's eldest son

Dorothea C.M. Oliver, Nov 1877
Daughter of Celia Oliver (née
Gowlland)

I don't think any of us are tempted seriously to read through Oliver's Legal Work. I read the preface as soon as I received it and I was sorry that there was not more of the same kind of reading. How much I wish you could get something over here. It seems unnatural that we sh'd never see you. We must keep up our correspondence regularly.

> Lakeside, Churchfield
> Road, Ealing W.
> 30 October 79

My dearest Birdie,

Many thanks for y'r long letter dated 31st. August. I am very ashamed of my poor little letters when I read your long ones. The £5 also came safe to hand and I have already expended £2:2: of it according to your instructions in paper. It does not go so far as you expected however – the stamping is rather expensive in colour as you will see from the enclosed bill – the die had of course to be engraved for the address. Your old crest I had not lost and your envelopes will accordingly be stamped with the crest. If there is any money over after the latter costs have been paid for I will spend the balance on paper. They don't keep at the stores the small fancy paper and envelope combined which you ask me to get.

Pages two and three of this letter are missing.

…a year so we have very little fear of damp; on wet evenings a little moisture appears on some of the walls but otherwise the place is very dry. The soil is gravel with a stratum of sand beneath. Rain of which we have so much here in England therefore disappears as soon as it falls. These are all advantages.

The drawbacks are that the house is not very solidly built –
speculator Builder's work in fact – and one's mind cannot be
quite at rest as to its stability. Everybody tells me however it will
last my time. I therefore try to forget possible Builder's Bills in
the future and murmur to myself apres moi le deluge. We have
90 years lease and 10£ ground rent the interest of purchase
money £34 a year. Rates and Taxes about double what we paid
before. It will be a tight fit to make £400 a year meet all the
expenses. Having an unfortunate prejudice for paying my bills I
am not without some apprehension that there may be a
difficulty in keeping up this practice. But we have burnt our
bridges now and it is no good repining. If we don't get along we
shall have to get in a lodger and indeed have had a good deal of
thought of taking in Percy Whitcombe and another hospital
student to get some money! This is not a cheerful prospect but
que voulez vous one can't have everything and the man who is
rash enough to marry on a small income must be prepared to put
up with some inconvenience to enjoy the luxury of a little wife
and little Bairns. You see with the selfishness for which men are
proverbial I don't mention what that little wife may have to put
up with if the said students shall invade us.

Trot has been spending 14 days with us. She left today to
stay with the Hewitts. She seems very well again now - works a
great deal too hard and makes herself quite tired every evening.
She is a charming person and as good and generous as it is
possible to be. One of the most unselfish of women I sh'd say –
always bright and cheerful. If only her husband were bearable
she w'd have every reason to be so for her children are
perfection. Percy whom we see a good deal of is a charming
young fellow. He has just taken another laurel at his hospital. He
has been selected after examination of all the second year
students to the post of Prosector, which carries a small payment

and is considered a great distinction being given to the best student and most promising surgeon among the students.

I have a severe cold and headache this evening, which will excuse my incoherence in this letter. We have had very little sleep again lately. The dear old Peeps has had an attack of croup and still has a bad cough. We only had about 3 hours sleep last night; for 4 hours he was coughing almost incessantly. He has not been out for a fortnight and looks very white indeed. The little Bobs as we call her had a bad cold too but she is so strong that it doesn't seem to affect her very much. She still can't talk at all but she understands all she is told I think. She is very fond of the Peeps and he of her. He pushes her over rather unceremoniously but flies into a violent passion if any one else ventures to reprove her. She never complains or cries at his rough treatment but if he is in trouble she begins to whimper at once. She is not fond of being kissed and will only hold up her face when I have my hat on to go away to London. The boy is most affectionate and is genuinely delighted to romp with me. He adopts all Jessie's pet expressions. This evening he said when we were sitting alone here together "Let me sit on your lap you dear old man and look at some pictures". He is very proud of his cough and when the Bobs was being held up to him as the pattern of good behaviour the other day he said "Ah! But she can't cough" !!

I am sorry to hear what you report of Mrs. Fred. But I am hardly surprised at anything of that kind that I hear now. One is always hearing of scandals nowadays – I suppose the world has always been much the same; but from the little I have seen of men and women I sh'd say that Society is much worse than it used to be. People relate to you nowadays all sorts of scandals and intrigues as a matter of course, which would have been spoken of in a whisper or not mentioned at all a few years ago. Anyone reading the so-called Society Journals must notice this.

All the same a good wide margin must be allowed for exaggeration in all such matters. People are too prone to put the worst construction on anything which would offend ones friends and so very innocent flirtations are magnified into serious scandals if married women are concerned in them. It is safe to believe only half one hears in such matters.

The Joscelynes have had a little luck. The old Rector of Ibstone who retired taking 1/5 of the stipend as R. died the other day and so Henry gets all the salary attached to the cure at £395 a year. He has one pupil who pays him £100 a year.

Mary Joscelyne has been very dangerously ill. Heart disease apparently – an attack brought on by hard reading for the Cambridge Local Examinations. She is at home and will be obliged to remain there for a long time apparently. Harry Joscelyne is still at his post in Scotland (at Perth) where he is tutor in a school.

Annie keeps pretty well. She is up at the Refuge Pimlico taking the place of someone who is away for 3 weeks holiday. She came down for my birthday the 26th. I am just turned 34 and am feeling much older than I used to think men of that age ought to feel. However I have everything about me to keep me young. Jessie is quite well and sends her love to you both. Kiss all the dear children for us. With best love to Alick, believe me your most affectionate R.S.G.

1880

15 January 1880

Fancy our dear little Peeps acted in a play the other day before 80 people. He had only one sentence to say on stage but he had to wait some time for his cue and we quite expected he would miss it; but he didn't, saying what he had to say with the greatest earnestness and very naturally. Indeed of all the children on the stage (and he was only half the age of the youngest) he seemed to pay the greatest attention to what was going forward and to enter into the thing. When they all went off the stage each child thinking of course of how to get off best he was left alone standing with his legs apart staring at the people very much to every one's amusement and only toddled off when he was called from the flys. He was quite the hero of the evening everyone wanting to talk to him as he was the hero. The party was at the house of Jessie's cousin Mrs Leach who lives in London. There was a dance afterwards of grown up people. The Peeps had never seen dancing before and was deeply interested and of course had to have a dance himself. What struck him most was the flying of the tails of the men's coats as they whirled round – this he thought a very remarkable and noticeable phenomenon!!! He slept in the house and went off quite good to bed at 8 o'clock and slept like a top in spite of the noise. Jessie saw him to bed and he added of his own a word to his little prayers this little thanksgiving "And thank God for my nice party."

We have all been remarkably well I am thankful to say in spite of a most severe winter - the coldest December in England this century. The people were skating for three weeks on end, the ice 6 or 7 inches thick. Our house being a new one too and the walls not too thick it is quite a mercy that none of us have had colds or rheumatism. When the thaw came our walls were quite dripping with wet but then fortunately we were all at Gravesend spending Xmas. That went off very well the Lakes all being very amicable. We saw all we could of Trot and her boys.

Agnes Elizabeth Mary Alleyne, 4½ years

Nona Lake, June '77

She is just going to Southampton for three months to take charge of Mrs Cooper. The old Lady is quite out of her mind on one point and one only and that is that it is her duty to give all her money away to beggars. This has become so serious – thousands of pounds having been squandered – that it has become necessary to remove her from Brighton, where the beggars reside, to some other place. Southampton has been selected as being the residence of relations of hers and she is to be there in lodgings and Trot is to be with her to see that she receives and sends out no letters and sees no one. Trot is to have all the money and is to be paid at the rate of £100 a year for her services while she is actually with her. She will take 3 months and then go home while Cooper takes charge. The old lady has managed all the family affairs for a long time past 20 years and Cooper and his brother have both been too idle to look into matters – when he did so at last a couple of months ago he found the affairs in the greatest confusion and had reason…

…stage…(? one should not) despair of being of some use to a man however much he may object to be helped. I am afraid you have put yourself out of court regards this matter. I wish Oliver had received…

Lakeside.
Churchfield Road.
Ealing

4th March 1880

My dearest Celia,

Your latest photographs arrived this evening following your letters of 19th January rec'd. this morning, together with Oliver's. I am very glad he has not entirely given me up. I see he

says he is 46: well, if ever I get to that great age – it doesn't seem
so great though as it did a few years ago – I can foresee that if my
present laziness in the matter of letter writing continues I shall
be a much worse correspondent than he is – for I think he does
send me a letter say once in two years. The truth is, I suppose,
that as one grows older one feels more and more the futility of
the world. There is so little that ever occurs to one that seems
worth mentioning. Nothing certainly ever occurs to me which I
consider worth recording. When I am about to write to you, for
instance, I always feel inclined to get out the last good book I
have read and copy out for you what I approve of, adding merely
that "these are my sentiments" only expressed far better than I
can do. Here for instance is something that has been ringing in
my ears for some days past. I say the words over and over to
myself and (? gain relief in turn) –

For ever and for ever
The eternal mountains rise
And lift the virgin snows on high
To meet the silent skies
And shall this soul which measures all
Like these stand steadfast, sink & fall?

For ever and for ever
The changeless oceans roar
And dash their thundering surges down
Upon the sounding shore;
As this swift soul; this lightning will,
Shall these, while they roll on, be still?

For ever & for ever
The swift suns roll through space
From age to age they wax & wane,

Each in its ordered place;
Yet shall this soul, whose inner eye
Foretells their cycles, fade & die?

For ever & for ever
We have been, and we are,
Unchanging as the ocean waves
Unresting as the star.
Though suns stand still, & time be o'er
We are, & shall be, evermore.

We like the photographs very much; but if I had seen it in a strange album I w'd not have known you. Your face has altered, your expression has altered, your figure has altered. I suppose if I were to meet you in the street I would not know you in the least. I see in you face a great likeness to Louisa only you are much better looking. Jessie, on the other hand, says you are the image of Trot, which I can't see at all. That photograph of Trot taken with Miss Niorson, by the way, is quite the best portrait I have seen of Trot – it is a speaking likeness.

Talking of Trot, there have been squalls at Gravesend touching a dressmaker bill of £26, all the (?debt) Trot has had chargeable to her husband for 4 years – (he)was summoned to County Court and, not defending the suit, was condemned to pay. A judgement summons was got up by the dressmaker which he did not attend to. He was had up again and committed for contempt of Court to 40 days imprisonment. He swore to the Judge he w'd not pay but would go to prison – wanted to know whether he sh'd give himself up at once. The judge said time w'd be given him to think better of it. He went home and was about to resign all his appointments and give up his practice. This of course w'd be the ruin of the Boys so I at once wrote to old Lake, who kept me informed (in Trot's absence at Bournemouth with

Mrs. Cooper), that I would pay. In the meantime Harry Whitcombe had heard of it and taken out of his Savings Bank a sum of £30, which he won as scholarship at Epsom 4 or 5 years ago, and with this and some money he borrowed, paid the bill, now swollen with costs to £34. So there is an end of the matter for the present except that of course the money must be made good to Harry. I sent Percy down to see his father and persuade him not to give up his practice and to this he seems to have consented. His public appointments amount to £500 a year. He seemed to be much relieved to find the Bill had been paid and he was not to go to prison. But he w'd certainly have gone rather than pay. A more accomplished maniac it is impossible to imagine.

We do pity you when we hear of your servant difficulties. It is dreadful to think of all the changes you have. I don't know of anything more wearing than that of domestic difficulty – except perhaps for a wife who beats one! Or is a fool – which could be even worse. By the way, I am rather surprised that you have never said another word about your controversy with Fred and how it ended – I sh'd like to know.

Tell Oliver he paid me double or treble the worth of the Blue Books I sent him long ago. But if he still feels indebted to me and wishes to ease his conscience let him get a cabinet photograph of himself and send me to pair yours.

That dear boy of yours is my great delight. Do keep a little record of his little ways for me. He is a glorious fellow. I can promise you he and I would be tremendous friends. I am quite expecting to hear he has run away in search of adventures. Two little cousins (boys) of Jessie's aged 7 and 8, Mrs. Leach's children, ran away from home the other day. Instead of going to the Kindergarten Day School which they attend, they packed up in their little book knapsacks what they considered all the necessities of travel, a bit of soap, toothbrush, clean collars, prayer book and bible and trudged off to the country – weren't missed till dinner time, of course and then all the Police were informed and they were found towards evening, having walked 16 miles and dined off a pennyworth of nuts!! They had proposed to sleep under a hedge and would give no explanation to the Policeman who found them or to their Parents when they got home except that "It was a call from God"!!! It was at their house that the Peeps acted this winter. Did I tell you? He had only one line to say and to our great surprise and delight he waited for his cue and said what he had to say in the most natural way when the piece was over and all the other children walked off the stage, no one thinking of him, he remained all alone there staring at the 80 people who were looking on – to their great amusement – until he was called off. I have no doubt I have told you all this before and how when he said his prayers that night he added "and thank God for my nice party". Both our little pets are too charming. They are the greatest delight to us both. I must tell you of the Kit's first sentence. She came up to me the other day and looking up with her great blue eyes in my face said "Scatch me" (scratch me)!!!! She is a tough little creature; has great tumbles and never cries or minds a bit. The Peeps is growing very nicely. He was not well the last time I wrote but he is better now and when he is well he is no trouble at all. He sleeps in our room and Kits with the nurse overhead. We have had all good nights lately. He is taking a teaspoonful of cod liver oil at night now and it seems to do him good. He takes it in orange wine and quite likes it. Kits has never wanted any medicine since she was born.

Annie is staying at Fordham near Cambridge with Mrs Woodgate and seems to be in clover. They appear to live very comfortably. It is a great relief to us when she is away – we much prefer to be alone. Poor old thing, she does make such silly remarks. It quite irritates me – especially when she has come from the Sisters this is the case. One gets so sick of hearing all the tittle tattle which she retails of their proceedings. We have to hear what she has had for dinner and tea and supper!! She has a most unfortunate talent for picking on all the most uninteresting features of her experiences for conversation. It is difficult to make you understand what I mean but here is an illustration – you sent us the review of Alec's book. I told her she would not care to read it at which she expressed great indignation and forthwith mounted her spectacles and squared down to it and read it all through, never uttering a sound until she reached the end when she said "Ha – the paper is thin but strong with a beautiful smooth surface; the type is exceedingly clear"!!!!!!!! Poor Jessie and I almost rolled off our chairs! That was her solitary comment.

Adieu, my dearest Birdie – Best love to Oliver and see if you can't get him photographed for us. Kiss all your darlings for us. Ever your most affectionate, RSG.

24 March. With, I hope unusual stupidity, I left this letter at home on the mail day so have had to keep it for the Frisco route. I have since received your letter and the enclosed £5 - of which £3:9: only belongs to me. The rest I will treat as a deposit account. I was very sorry to send the Box per the Lusitania but Mrs. Lucas wrote and begged me to send the clothes at once or they w'd arrive too late for the summer wear and would afterwards be too small for Marcius. I am sorry the carriage was so heavy. I can't imagine that in any circumstances it can pay to get things from here unless you can get them taken out here for nothing. Harry Whitcombe came to see me today. He has just taken the first prize in mathematics at Winchester. He is therefore top boy at mathematics in the whole school and is pretty secure of a New College scholarship next year. Trot has been very ill with inflammation of windpipe but is now better.

All those operations have left her extremely delicate. We are in
the middle of Electioneering here. There is an universal belief
that the Conservatives will come in again with a huge majority.
Do you remember you were at Gravesend during the last
Election 6 years ago and Jack and I attended the meetings? Poor
old Jack was very disgusted with the Liberal ?Candidate… he
based this on an instinct that… I am voting for the Liberals and I
heartily hope they will have a big win. When this reaches you,
you will know*

HM Office of Works,
Whitehall.
9 April 80

Dearest Birdie,

Just a line to tell you that we have another little daughter –
born last Sunday morning at 3 o'clock – 4 April the feast of St.
Ambrose. Don't you think we ought to call her Ambrosia? Jessie
has been and is remarkably well. We have had a homeopathic
Doctor whose treatment is just directly opposite to the received
canons which govern affairs in such circumstances. For instance
the day the baby came he ordered eggs and bacon for Jessie's
breakfast beef tea at 11 and roast beef and vegetables with stout
at one o'clock for dinner!! She has obeyed all his instructions

---

* The Liberals won and Gladstone became Prime Minister for the second time.
The appointment of George John Shaw Lefevre as First Commissioner of
Works (the Minister responsible for the Department of Public Building and
Works) led to an upturn in Richard's fortunes. GJ Shaw Lefevre (b. 1832)
came from a noted parliamentary family and served as a middle-ranking
Minister in both Gladstone's administrations. He was created Baron Eversley
for services to the Liberal Party in 1906.

and has as I said continued very well indeed. She is to sit up next Sunday.

The baby is a charming little creature I am told! She certainly is more presentable than our other babies have been – is very quiet and good and sleeps continually.

Trot came up to see Dr. Mackenzie about her throat which has been bad – inflamed windpipe. He did her good and she is gone back to Bournemouth. I dined at the Hewitts on Tuesday – they had a great baptism party. Trot is Godmother – Mrs. Fox and a schoolfellow of Jessie's, a Miss Freeman, and Percy Whitcombe are the appointed Godparents of our baby. She will be called Josephine Mary. Josephine after Mrs. Fox.

So my prediction in my last letter to you has come true and we are going to have a Liberal Government – for which I am thankful.

Adieu best love to Oliver. Ever yr. afft. R.S.G.

Just had a long letter from Fred with Cabinet photographs of his two girls. Odd that his boy and mine were born the same day 14th Dec. Odd too that you and I each have two girls and a boy. I hope yr. infants are well.

12 Whitehall Place,
21/5/80

My dearest Birdie,

Your commands for more paper will be obeyed. We have had a fire at the C.S. Stores and there is confusion there at present but in a few days I will order the paper. I despair of sending it out cheaply however. The man I know at Greens could only send out free quite a small parcel such as a book or two he told me.

Jessie and the new baby are fairly well. I say fairly because the new baby doesn't grow much and is not quite so lively as the other infants have been except in the matter of crying. The others are very well indeed and great sport. I had 'em all three romping with me at seven o'clock this morning. They are both charmed with the new Baby and treat her with the greatest gentleness. I am afraid Jessie won't be able to keep up with the nursing. She complains a good deal of giddiness this time. So we shall have to go with artificial food. What an astonishing thing it is that after the birth of such myriads of millions of human beings it should still remain an open question what is the right and proper food to give to a young infant!

Trot is just coming home leaving Lilly Joscelyne in charge of Mrs Cooper. Louisa was here the other day and I had a grand field day into her on the subject of her family. They all think too much of themselves and I ventured to tell her so. It was quite a revelation to her and she indignantly repudiated it. She was so angry that I quite expect we shall hear no more of her. Percy Whitcombe is here chattering to me so that I can't write any more. He has just made 122 runs in a cricket match and is more proud than if he had taken the greatest scholarship in the world.

Adieu, best love to Oliver and kisses to (the) chicks.

Ever yr. afft. R.S.G.

                                        12 Whitehall Place.
                                        4 June 1880

My dearest Birdie,

Still no news going here but you will be expecting to hear from me nevertheless.

Jessie and the new baby have not been as well as I w'd wish. The baby doesn't grow is white and pasty and cries too much and sleeps too little and is always sick too. We have a Homeopathic Dr. who gives her half a pilule of Ipecacuanha three times a day and for severe (?fretiness) a pilule of Chamomilla. (He is) giving Jessie tonics but hitherto they don't seem to have done much for her. Of course the baby's and her seediness act and react on each other as the baby is being nursed.

Edward and Kitty are very well, barring a small skin rash. They spend a great deal of time with me. Kitty is getting very affectionate. She used to be (a) cold-hearted little creature like you were when you were a baby! She reminds me continually of you. She and Edward claw each other's hair often and I am bound to say Edward generally comes off second best. Kitty's teeth are her reserve when hostilities are very much in earnest. The poor old Peep's arms a scarred with the marks of her little bites! She is the piggy of the family. She can always dispose of anything that is offered to her – sweets cake jam beef all together if necessary! When I come home they always come out to me in the garden for an hour and we garden together and Kitty goes round to "snell" (smell) every individual flower. They are very fond of grubbing and making a mess and no amount of scolding will induce them not to rake the borders into the path! We have just laid in a roller and a mowing machine. Whenever either is in operation I have one child hanging to each side!

Annie is away with her friend at the present moment and a great calm seems to (?reign) in the house. Trot spent a night with us on her way home from Bournemouth. She seemed by no means well and looked pale and worn. Her throat is her weak point. Not the swollen gland per se, but general weakness. She will be at home now until the winter when I hope she will get away from Gravesend again. All the Doctors seem to think it would be dangerous for her to spend a winter at Gravesend.

Of Louisa and her family we never hear anything.

Percy Whitcombe dined here the night before last. It was his 21st birthday. He had that day received his prizes at the Hospital. He took three for Anatomy, Botany and Organic Chemistry. Lord Carnarvon gave the prizes away. You will see a report of the proceedings and Percy's name in yesterday's Times. In the Times however they give him one prize only instead of 3. He is captain of the Hospital Cricket Club and he has two matches about per week which I am glad of for he is inclined to work too much.

Jessie was trying to intimidate Edward the other day with the police. He explained that the Force had no terrors for him. He was on the best of terms with them. "We know a policeman Kitty and I, he always comes to talk to us. He has curly hair. He likes Alice too (Alice is the nurse). He calls her my darling"!!

Well goodbye. Best love to Oliver and kisses to yourself and the Bairns.

Ever yr. afft. R.S.G.

12 Whitehall Place SW.
10 Sep. 80

My darling Birdie,

I am ashamed when I think of the long time which has elapsed since I last wrote to you. I dare say tho' you have not observed it – you have been passing through such a string of events. I was indeed sorry to hear of all the stress you have had, and very much both Jessie and I wished that we could have been near you at such a time to lend you a hand. I am afraid you must be quite worn out – and yet no one but yourself could have done so much for the poor little baby. I am sure you ought to have a

gold medal for saving life. I am the more impressed with such
perseverance because we have just seen a case at Brighton in
which a baby just the age of yours was allowed o die – simply as I
believe because it was left to nurses and the mother did not give
it any personal attention. I hope and trust that you are long since
out of the wood and that we shall hear good news next mail.
Thank Oliver very much from me for his letters. I wish I had the
energy to set to work and write to him too but I become more
idle as the years go on, I am afraid. The whole time I was on leave
at Brighton I abjured from pen and ink entirely and that is why I
didn't at once write to congratulate you as I do now upon the
birth of your new daughter. When I think of all the trouble we
had to keep our sweet boy alive and of all the joy and happiness
we have had and have in possessing him I am inclined to think
that "Detropa"!!!* will be found after a very brief acquaintance to
belie her name entirely. All our pets are very well. Kittens is
coming on nicely – walks and talks a great deal. I carried her a
good many miles at Brighton when we were on leave. I used to
spend the whole day with the Brats on the beach or taking them
donkey rides or goat chaise rides or walks – and very much they
appreciated it. So when there was talk of going away back to
Ealing the Peeps added a little petition to his prayers that he
might be allowed to remain at Brighton or Bwiton as he calls it
for he doesn't pronounce his rs at all well.

Your box per Mr. L. Mann has just arrived here and before I
add another word I shall proceed to unpack it. All safe I find
except one pot of jelly, which is smashed. Thanks for these. The
infants will all bless you! One box containing 6 knives and 6
forks to be resilvered – and a blue coat for Tomkins. I wish you
had got his address. I haven't it I am afraid but I will see among

*   Too Much. The baby was christened Helen Ruth.

my papers. I asked young Mann to dinner but he wrote back that the ship is being got ready for sea and he can't get leave.

I went down to see Annie today a t Pimlico. She has just come back from Ibstone. She doesn't seem to hit it off with Louisa and the family; they are always pecking at her, poor old soul and trying to depreciate the Whitcombes – it seems! Henry Joscelyne has just obtained another tutorship at a school at Tunbridge Wells. He got very good testimonials from his last employers. I like him. He seems a very honest manly fellow – very quiet but I sh'd say very determined – and very gentlemanlike in every way. He still has an idea of going to Australia. I dare say he will turn up one day at Shelcote! He is going to try to get a Bible Clerkship at All Souls in the autumn. Goodbye my dearest Birdie. With best love to you and…Oliver and thousands of kisses to your babies. R.S.G.

Ministry of Works
6th December 1880

My dearest Birdie,

Jessie was abusing me last night for my long silence to you-wards and was informing me that the whole blame of my remissness in this particular would be laid upon her shoulders. Louisa already charges her, I hear, with being the insinuator of building up a great wall of ice between my relations and me. If such an idea sh'd enter your head I pray you to set it aside at once. My own laziness is the only cause to be assigned. There seems to be so little news that I have not had the courage to sit down and write you a letter. It is impossible that you should become excited about the baby's teeth and Edward's falls and Kitty's tears and laughter – and these and nothing else make up our domestic talk and beyond domestic talk we have nothing to report. At least until Friday last there was nothing else, but then I was made Private Secretary to the First Commissioner of Works, Mr. Shaw Lefevre, the Political head of my Department – and thereupon I resolved that you sh'd have a letter by next mail to report this fact and any others I could rake together, You will be glad of this promotion. Of course, Private Secretaries go out with their Chiefs and so from a pecuniary point of view it is not so important. But it is supposed to confer a great deal of social distinction to be private secretary to a minister and so I call upon you to rejoice with me. Of course it will give me a lot more work to do but I don't mind in the least.

Jessie and the babies are well. The latest born, Miriam Josephine, is a duck. The most perfect little pet it is possible to imagine – and the least trouble of our children – indeed she is no trouble at all. Her little life has been one long happiness to herself and all about her. She has only just cut her first tooth. She is going on for 9 months old – Jessie is still nursing her but will have to give that up before very long I imagine. I hope your little flock is quite well. We saw the photographs you sent to Annie the other day. She is back with us again after spending a long time away with the Sisters and with the Sister in charge of the Refuge. Dr. Mackenzie tells Trot that when he examined her the other day he found her heart disease had made no advance. She seems very well indeed and complains less than most people do – but nevertheless her heart is so unsound that she might be taken off any minute. She herself hasn't the least notion of this – which is a great blessing for her. Trot has just come up to see the Dr. She hasn't been well again. I dined with the Hewitts (on Saturday night) with whom she's staying. Percy is living at Ealing with old Mrs. Whitcombe, Mrs. Hewitt's mother, who recently lost her husband and has a larger house than she wants. They are living only a couple of hundred yards from us and so we see a good deal of Percy. He is getting along famously at his

October 1878

hospital and I think will make a good Doctor. Harry Whitcombe is so far recovered from the scarlet fever that he is expected home in 10 days. Dr. Ridding told his father when he was recently at Winchester that there is no doubt about his getting a scholarship at New College. He will be going there next year.

I never hear any news of Fred. Do you? I don't know that I feel nothing but regret at the proposed marriage of Jack's widow. She is such a weak silly woman that it can only be gain to her children to get a stepfather provided he treats them with decent kindness – and that I hope may be expected from the sort of man whom you describe.

Jessie's father has been very ill - he doesn't take the least care of himself – eats nothing and drinks a great deal for a man who doesn't eat – the result is that he has all the symptoms of a man who is breaking up. Mary Lake, who can't stand Gravesend in the winter, is spending the winter with us. We are paid what she costs us – and as she is a good quiet little creature the arrangement is a pleasant one.

Well goodbye – I shall send you a paper announcing my appt. It gives me £100 a year extra by the way. With my best love to Oliver who I hope is flourishing and love to the Bairns – believe me always yr. afft. R.S.G.

I am just going to send your forks & knives to you. I am going to examine in German the girls of St. John's School this Xmas.

                                        12 Whitehall Place S.W.
                                        30 Dec.1880

My dearest Birdie,

Continually the spirit moves me to sit down and write to you but as often the weary man replies – yes but what have you got to say? And so for that time the matter is postponed. You are very good at writing to me. Your long letters are our greatest delight and we appreciate them the more because it is clear that you are just about as occupied with your domestic affairs as Jessie is. She keeps up a large correspondence. I am ruined with the demand for postage stamps. She has really much less spare time than I have and yet I find myself constantly throwing my letters over to her to answer. It is for conduct like this that men have earned for themselves the reputation of unbounded selfishness.

We drank all your healths on Christmas day and wondered whether you were bathing or picnicking or yachting or what. We were freezing – up to Xmas the weather had been warm as June. But at 7 o'clock on Xmas morning when Jessie and I turned out to go to church the ground was iron bound and we had the pleasure of being able to cross the road without the time worn joke in reference to the employment of a boat. For ours is a new road and not yet submitted to steam rollers, wood pavements and asphalt (wood pavements for the main roads and asphalt for the foot paths are being introduced everywhere now) and we have trouble to get across in wet weather. We made this Xmas a day of feasting for the children. They began with stockings filled with presents from Santa Claus – too many sweets among them which resulted in an inability to do justice to the plum pudding when it arrived - and we had all the romps we could find breath for from morning to night. Annie was with us. She went up to St. Barnabas for the service but turned up in time for dinner. Our services at Ealing were more than usual satisfactory. At the Christmas Eve service and at the afternoon service we had Christmas Carols sung and sung very well. The Choir at our Church has improved of late and if we could only improve the sermon we would feel very happy on this score. The last two Sundays Jessie and I have been up to St. Pauls in the afternoon to hear Canon Liddon preach. The crowd to hear him is so great that it was on each occasion necessary to take up a position at the door half an hour before they were opened and 1 ¼ hours before the beginning of the service. We did that on each occasion and were rewarded with excellent places just under the middle of the dome. In five minutes after the doors were opened the whole of the dome and part of the nave were crammed with people. The waiting was amply rewarded by Liddon's magnificent sermons. I don't think you ever heard him. He always seems to me as much head and shoulders above the ordinary good preacher as Patti's and Neillson's* singing is above the ordinary drawing room performances. On both occasions the sermon lasted 50 minutes. The attention of the congregation never once flagged – among the thousands of listeners you might almost hear a pin drop and I did not notice that a single individual went out before the end. In both sermons there were very pointed allusions to the injustice, the impolicy and the want of all real Christianity for shutting men up in prison for questions of Conscience. Liddon indeed has all through taken up the cause of the imprisoned Ritualists as they are called rather warmly, and each of his sermons this month – he is Canon in Residence a month at a time every three months – has been directed more or less to this matter. On the 26th i.e. last Sunday we dropped in at All Saints on the way to St. Pauls. The music there has been worked up to the highest pitch of perfection.

My Baby has two teeth both below. I think she must be cutting some more for she has been unusually restless and wakeful of late for the first time since she was born. How many teeth has your baby? Our Kitty is a pretty little round-faced baby with great blue round eyes which seem to look out wonderingly at you always. She is very independent – rather prefers little games she can play with by herself, and if several small children

---

*   Christina Nilsson and Adelina Patti were the two most famous sopranos of
      the day.

are in the nursery she tires very soon of the noise and the romping and asks to be allowed to be taken up to the "Dining Wrnoom". Edward on the other hand is never more happy than when he has a crowd around him. As he leads in his own nursery he always expects to do so wherever he is – it is amusing to see him patronising little girls double his age! He has a great sense of his own dignity. When I sent him to ask whether I was soon going to have some tea and his nurse said "Certainly I was going to have some tea at once" he came to me in high dudgeon repeated to me what had been said "I call it very rude of Alice don't you " he said! He is very impatient of Kitty's being corrected – always flies into a passion about it. The other day Kitty was not quiet at prayers and was put in my little room for punishment. He kept quite quiet till prayers had been begun again then he burst out "You naughty girl mother to shut up my little sister" then burst into tears and threw himself on the floor. He is himself a very good little fellow – very obedient and unselfish. I took him into a shop and bought a stick of chocolate intending it for himself but he at once broke it in two and put half in his pocket for Kitty and carried it safely about all the morning untouched. He looks very white. Kitty is round and pink. She eats a great deal more than she does. We are giving them both a teaspoon full of Cod Liver Oil every afternoon now.

It was extremely kind of you and Oliver to send the dear old Peeps such a handsome present. He will soon be the richest member of the family in these Islands. About that paper. I am sorry the Stores did not send some note. Whatever you told me to order I ordered because I handed them you letter to take the order from. They explained to me I remember that as the money to be spent was limited to £2 they would not be able to send much, if any note of them. I am afraid no good would come of my raising the question now more particularly as the dies have been sent to Australia - at least that I presume since they have not been sent to me. I have got your knives and forks and am going to try to get them sent out free per Orient Line as soon as I can get away into the City. But my time now is so occupied that although the plate has been here some time I have not been able to see about sending it.

My new appt. gives me long bursts of work from time to time and then I have comparatively little or nothing to do; but even then I am obliged to be here to hear any orders my chief has to give. I go away from home at the usual time and generally get back 2 or 3 hours later than I used to. My Chief's principal work and therefore mine has nothing whatever to do with Works and Pub. Bldngs. He is the great authority in England on the Land question especially on the Irish Land question and as an Irish Land Bill is impending you can imagine that there is plenty of work to do.

My best love to Oliver - kiss the dear children for me – and with best love to yourself, believe me always your very afftn.R.S.G.

1881

Beatrix de Michele (née Lake)

Lakeside,
Churchfield Road,
Ealing.

23rd February 1881

My dearest Birdie,

You are evidently going to pay me back in my own coin, for having neglected you for many mails you are now neglecting me. I read in the papers about your lack of water and then of your great prosperity at the prorogation of y'r parliament the other day. So setting the one statement against the other, I conclude that you are not all round so badly off in New South Wales.

Our life is so uneventful that I am quite at a loss to tell you any news. Our baby, Miriam, has 8 teeth so Jessie tells me; for my own part I can only vouch for two, having never been able to find the other six. She is a most fascinating little baby – is just able to say "Mum" and "Dad" and "Addy" (the nurse), to wave her hand and to kiss. She sleeps all night now, and comes down to us from the nursery at 8 o'clock when she sits up and eats a biscuit till her milk is got ready for her. Kittens also appears at the same time all dressed, and generally amuses herself emptying everything on the dressing table – purses, pots, ring stands, etc. till she is carried off to breakfast. Edward now sleeps in the dressing room adjoining us and as soon as day begins to dawn he is shouting out enquiries as to whether it is morning. He is invariably told that it is not, whereupon he gets up and seizes biscuits which are left on his table, and a book to amuse himself in his bed for an hour or two. Then he creeps in to us and we tell him stories till the other two children appear. Then he is dressed by his mother and they all three pack off to the nursery. Jessie always gets up about 7 or 7.30. I never do till 8 or later. I hate getting up and only degree less hate going to bed. I have to leave home at 9.15 to catch my train and so reach my office at 10.30 walking 3 miles from Paddington to Whitehall. My chief doesn't usually arrive till 12.0 so I have time to read my newspapers. I have to read 6 every day / and cut out all that concerns him and this Dept. before he arrives. I also have to read through the Votes & Proceedings of Parliament and get ready the replies to any questions he has to answer. Then I am usually kept here till 5 or 6 doing the thousand and one things a private secy. has to get through; but mostly I have to carry home – and do before morning – drafts of confidential memoranda of which I have to make fair copies. It takes a heap of time and as one has to write very legibly is very tiresome. I haven't had to go down to the House yet – but I daresay I shall have to when our Estimates come out.

Jessie celebrated yesterday her 25th birthday. She is very well & cheerful as usual. We have been having a brief period of Elysium lately for we have been quite alone. Annie is at Gravesend staying with Trot and Mary Lake is gone away for no time to be bridesmaid at a wedding. Annie has also been spending a few days with Mrs. Busbridge at Malling. She appears to be fairly well and Trot too seems to be getting through this most severe winter wonderfully well. None of our contemporaries ever experienced such weather. The snow was so bad that one week more of it would have starved London; as it was there was no communication beyond Reading to the West for days and one of our two lines to Ealing was blocked up. The snow penetrated through every crack however small and the servants were engaged a greater part of the day carrying off what drifted through crevices and keyholes. I was agreeably surprised on coming home that Tuesday – the day of the worst snowstorm seen here for 10 years – to find the house standing. One bedroom window had been blown in and before I got home no end of snow had got into the room in spite of all their efforts to bring up the window. The children alone thoroughly enjoyed themselves! We were moreover frozen out of water for about 10 days. A good many people were killed by the weather. Among others Gould of Earsdon Vicarage at the age of 44. Of my old friend Younghusband, I hear he is obliged to spend the winter at Malta and seems to get no better there, is as his sister tells me, fading away. Nettie, the youngest of the girls, married a Capt. in the 3rd Regt. about a year ago. She is staying in town and is going to dine with us on Monday. The third girl, Alice, is also married to a Capt. in the Army, so they have done very well I think. I may between this and Thursday, when the mail goes out, have something to add. If not, Goodbye. Best love to Oliver and the chicks (to whom I have sent, with your knives and forks, some picture books). A friend has promised to forward them per oriental line free.Ever yr. afft. R.S.G.

11 March 1881

My dearest Birdie,

I was delighted to get your long letter this morning and to hear good news of you all. It was very pleasant too to hear that Jack's children are going on well and that you like them. I am sure I hope Jennie will be happy with her new husband – but for my own part I can't say I have ever been able to whip up any interest in her proceedings. I am so glad you like Maudie and are able to praise her. Jack used to talk most of her and was evidently very devoted to her. I often wish I could be where it would be possible to see something of his children on that account as well as that I might see you again. I often form plans for going to Australia. But as I grow older and the family increases it seems a more and more remote and impracticable scheme. Just fancy a procession headed by Jessie and myself and finished by the 3 babies and nurse marching into Shelcots to take up quarters until something turned up! I feel sure I sh'd like Australia and that it would agree with us all better than this awful climate; and I don't hesitate to say that if I had a clear £300 a year to start with I would emigrate tomorrow. I quite dread the struggle our children will have in England in 20 years hence for bare existence. Even now there are armies of young men loafing about because it is impossible to find employment. All but the very clever go to the wall. So that if you don't see me you will probably see the Peeps in the next 15 years. He is still a most charming bright little fellow – full of life and fun and curiosity – above all curiosity. He insists on having everything explained to him. As the days are lengthening I get home in time to take him out before he goes to bed. He comes to help me in all the gardening operations and is a most pleasant little companion. Kitty is different in character altogether. She is fond of being alone and of playing little games of her own invention. If other children are in the house she rather avoids them. She and Edward are very good friends but he knocks her over rather unmercifully sometimes. He is very fond of arguing a point with the nurse and will keep up a fierce controversy for days, always repeating his original statement backed by new opinions on the subject which he collects from everyone in the house. His poor nurse is driven to desperation sometimes and threatens to terminate him. Then he is always correcting her English and tackles the opportunity of doing so always when Jessie or I am present! The young rascal. The little baby is a sweet loving little pet. She says "bye bye" to? adore, can crawl about, pull herself up to a chair - and sleeps from 9 till 6 without a break. She has brown eyes. The other two have blue. Annie is going on Thursday to be companion to a lady in Malvern Link – a friend of Cosby Whites – who as you know is ...and recommended Annie for this post. She is to go at first for a month on trial. The

Lady keeps a maid and wants A to read to her and drive with her. She is an invalid. I hope it will answer. She is to have £50 a year.

You don't owe me anything - au contraire I owe you £1 as shown below – RSG is

Dr. Cr.

0_1879

Oct. 20. Bill of Exchange 5. - . - . Oct. 23. Payment for Stationary. 2. 2 –

1880 Nov. 25. Tin-lined box for do. -. 11. 6

March. do. 5. - . - . 28. Tonkins bill. 5.11. -

Decr. do. 8. - . - . 1880

Jan.25. Stationary for Smarts. 2. - . - .

Dec. Resilvering plate 1.11. - .

do. Peeps Savings Bank 5. - . - .

1881

Feb.Parcel ticket 3/6 & Insurance 1/- -. 4. 6.

Balance due to Celia 1. - . - .

18. - . - . 18. - . - .

I enclose the ticket you will require to claim your parcel. I will keep the £1 till you want me to spend it here for you. I am getting on very well with my chief. I am just going to ask him to read Oliver's Preface on Land Registry & Transfer. Lefevre is the great reformer in these matters in England. He was chairman of the Parliamentary Committee of 77 on the subject. He has just re-published his report and other Essays in a book which he calls The English & Irish Land Questions.

Best love to Oliver & kisses to the babies. Ever yr. afft. R.S.G.

                                        Ealing
                                        10 August 1881

My dearest Birdie,

Thanks for your short letter. I congratulate you and Oliver on your access of fortune. If we had ourselves inherited a fortune, I don't think we should have been more pleased. It was certainly very handsome of Mr. Smart, having children of his own, to deal with you so generously. I have been abusing step-parents all my life but I think I shall now give it up.

Jessie and the infants are still in Brighton but return home on Saturday. I have been going down there from Saturday to Monday all the 9 weeks they have been there and this has kept off homesickness from which I always suffer if I am absent from Jessie and the chicks more than a week. They all look the picture of health and have I think enjoyed themselves very much. The baby who was in the Doctor's hands when they went there is now the most robust member of the party and walks about all day long. It was not 3 weeks ago that Edward walked ten miles with me without complaining of fatigue. Kittens celebrated her 3rd birthday last Monday. She approached the day with awe and wonder not knowing at all what it could mean or what was to happen to her. She had a great many presents and when she went to bed she enquired whether her birthday was now going away! Then she settled the difficult matter by declaring that she had her doll and her cradle and her little tin fishes and swans (all presents) downstairs and these were her birthday and these she sh'd always keep and so her birthday would be hers for ever. It sounds so like one of Hans Anderson's fairy tales or rather a bit of one.

Trot will probably tell you of Harry's success. He got a scholarship at New Coll. (£100), Exhibition from Winchester (50) equal to £150 for 5 years.

Trot went to Winchester to the ?Donium and to enjoy his triumph. He seems to have a great many friends at school and to be thoroughly liked by everybody. He goes up to Oxford in October. Percy has been less fortunate. He has just failed in his exam called 1st MB. It was not discreditable to him as it is an examination which men usually take up when they are qualified surgeons. He will not be qualified for a year to come...

> Lakeside, Churchfield
> Road, Ealing
> 21 Sept 1881

My dearest Birdie,

I do not seem to have written to you since you wrote commending Mr Bennett. I wrote to him to offer my services immediately and he called on me at my office, stayed, however only a few minutes then, and still fewer on a subsequent occasion when he called to ask a question with reference to a man with whom I had recommended him to place his son who is to be left in London to study medicine. I did my best but he evidently didn't want for friends over here – I tried to persuade him to come down to see us but he said he hadn't time. Before I left London, a few days before he was to sail, I wrote and said I w'd be happy to be of any use I could to his sons whom he leaves in London – to that letter I have had no reply but I hope he got it and a copy of Liddon's Bampton Lectures which I sent to him to be taken to you. This is a work I have myself read twice and

Jessie's mother and child? Eliza (née Neane)

Jessie Katharine Lake

mean to read again and again. It is the finest exposition of the whole scheme of the Church which I have ever come upon. I would like to think that you too had it at your finger ends. Here at any rate the air is thick with indifference to, if not openly expressed scorn of, the old truths – Liddon's setting them out are a refreshment and a delight to me as I hope they may be to you. Women happily for their own peace of mind are not so prone to be disturbed as men are by the prevailing "19th Century" free and easy spirit about religious questions. But in their case too it must be impossible for the foundations of belief to be too strongly and broadly laid.

Parliament was prorogued on the 26th August and my chief left Town leaving me to my own sweet will till November when he returns to work. I spent a fortnight with Cooper, a week at Bournmouth and a week at Brighton, very pleasantly. The Alleynes were at Brighton and I was really with them during the whole time of our stay there. Alleyne has charming little girls who became very soon my fast friends and indeed the nurse reported that a council had been held upon me and that the trio had unanimously resolved that if they were not already provided with a papa they would like to have me for one! They range from 7 to 10. Mrs Alleyne is a charming woman – very pretty too. They have a thousand a year to live upon and I don't know any people who manage to do so much with it - going abroad every other year for a 3 month expedition to Rome or elsewhere – leaving children at home – always going to the seaside or a farmhouse for a couple of the summer months – living in a comfortable house beautifully furnished – Alleyne seems to have an odd £100 or so to buy a picture or a statue with when he goes abroad – and giving the best dinner parties known to Exeter and also the most successful children's parties – dressing as Mrs Alleyne does too in the most strikingly perfect manner –

to accomplish all this and live within one's income I consider extremely clever.

Since my fortnight spent with Cooper I have been at home. Edward and I make an expedition somewhere almost every day. He is a capital walker and when he gets tired he perches on my shoulders. We went to the Zoo yesterday a long promised treat. He was immensely delighted but at first a little afraid of the big animals. The place has been immensely improved since I was last there 10 or 15 years ago. The old lion houses have been given up to bears and a grand new house erected where the lions and tigers prowl about among rocks and trees in huge enclosures like miniature crystal palaces. Edward had a ride on a camel and his only disappointment was that the elephant was not to be hired too. Like ourselves children evidently picture places to themselves before seeing them. He was filled with astonishment with the space and the flowers – which are really beautiful. He said "I was thinking last night that the Zoo would be a little square place with all the animals playing together in it!" he is a charming little companion now, taking a most intelligent interest in all he sees. Not the smallest part of the enjoyment yesterday was the ride on the top of the omnibus – when we reached our destination he said to me in the most serious tone of entreaty "Now do tell that conductor not to help me down" !! Kitty and the baby – so soon to be deposed! – are quite well and as merry little souls as it is possible to imagine. They all three play and laugh the whole day long. The baby is the tyrant of the nursery insisting on taking the principal part in every game that is played and overbearing all opposition with her teeth of which the other two stand in wholesome dread.

I went down to Ibstone on Friday returning on Saturday.

Whitehall Place.
4 Nov.81

My dearest Birdie,

I am rejoiced to hear of the birth of your second son and offer you both my warmest congratulations. Many thanks to Oliver for his letter. I am sorry that I can only announce a daughter. She came on 31st October; yours I take it was 31st August, so our new girl is two months younger than your new boy. Josephine was two months in advance of your dowager baby. She and Kitty are staying in London. Edward is gone to Norwood to stay with the Fox's two boys (8 and 5) – Mrs Fox writes this morning that he is rather homesick, and said he sh'd like to return home tomorrow, remarking that it was so much quieter at home. Of course his two little sisters are not quite so noisy as these two boys. The two girls are quite happy and show no signs of wishing to come back.

Annie came back after an absence of 7 months, a few hours after Mildred! She looks remarkably well and appears to be in the best of spirits. She has given up her old charge in Malvern.

I quite forget how recently I wrote to you and if I have told you I spent a week at Ibstone with the Joscelynes. I was extremely pleased with them – a more happy and united family it would be quite impossible to meet at all. Very badly off as usual of course; cela va sans dire. Joscelyne has a pupil at present but he leaves at Xmas. You might have a chance of recommending them a pupil. Australians coming here for education seem continually on the increase. Henry is a capital coach – a most conscientious old fellow which private coaches frequently are not. Herbert, the boy who is going to be a missionary, is a most charming fellow. He is just 17. The most clever boy is the next below him - Arthur who seems to be a case of old head on young shoulders. He is always setting the rest of the family right, possessing on occasions superior information! Alice I liked very much too. Poor Mary is a hopeless invalid, I am afraid. Dr Mackenzie who came to see her said she must be carried upstairs for the next year or so. Louisa seems better than ever and is usually the life and soul of the family.

You will be glad to hear that Jessie is doing remarkably well and is very pleased with her big fat baby. Goodbye. Best wishes to Oliver and kisses to you and the children. Ever your afft. R.S.G.

PS I went to the opening for a new chapel at Clewer on the 20th October for the House of Mercy. A most splendid edifice it cost £20,000. The Bishop in his sermon referred to the fact that the Community had had a great compliment paid them by Government. The Government has asked them to provide for the superintendence of a great hospital at Calcutta. They accepted the trust and the asst. Superior (who used to teach you music by the way) is going out tomorrow with two sisters to Calcutta.

1882–85

12 Whitehall Place SW.
27 January 82

My dearest Birdie,

   Thanks for your letter enclosing a Bill of Exchange for £20. I have told Trot of its arrival and will send her down cash for this am't next week by Percy. We were glad to have good news of you all – it is some time since you wrote. We don't believe in your method of managing Marcius – at least Jessie doesn't. I express no opinion. Her theory is that if he must be thrashed he sh'd be sent to school and thrashed there. I wonder what school you will send him to eventually. Whether you have any idea of sending him to school in England? We have had the Whitcombes a good deal this year. Not Trot, but Harry and Arthur. Harry spent 10 days with us. He continues to be a very pleasant fellow but his spirits are not as buoyant as they used to be I fancy and he looks pale and delicate – not the result of too much reading I fancy – more probably of too much smoking and song singing – the latter operation w'd not be performed by himself, since he is absolutely devoid of ear. Could not sing a recognizable stave of "God Save the Queen" I believe to save his life. Percy has more ear I believe. Curiously they are both tremendously fond of music. Percy will take great trouble to go to hear an oratorio standing half an hour outside the Albert Hall to secure a good place and toiling down to All Saints to church whenever he has a spare morning on Sunday. Harry is quite an authority on all the latest songs and their relative merit. Percy however will have to curb his love of ritual and fine music for the present. He has just been elected Ass't Surgeon of the Lock Hospital at Paddington and as such has to attend Chapel and appear in a sort of family pew every Sunday morning. Harry is gone back to Oxford where I hear he has the most elegant rooms it is possible to imagine filled with every luxury which Science and Art can

Jack and Percy   Jack? Richard?

devise. You have another nephew undergraduate at Oxford. Herbert Joscelyne matriculates there today. He is entered as an unattached student that being the cheapest method of obtaining a degree. It will not cost the Joscelynes much more than 70£ a year. Where however they are to find that amount I don't know. Just at the present moment they happen to be in clover – 3 new pupils unexpectedly coming to them. Annie is staying there just now. Percy and Harry went down last week to act Box and Cox at a party they gave. Harry Joscelyne was here yesterday – looked in to see me on the way from Dublin to Tunbridge Wells where he is still undermaster in a school. He is a great football player in a team* which has won a series of matches "cup-ties" which promises fair to all but beat All England. Trot always seems to be in hot water with her friend Mrs Hewett, who is a most offensive woman I think continually making mischief and setting people by their ears. I have been obliged to completely cut them, the Hewetts, in consequence. Poor Trot makes a great deal too much of these little quarrels. She seems to take a morbid interest in making the worst of things in general. I suppose this is the effect of bad health.

Jessie and I are going to a dance at Gravesend (the Rosherville Hotel) given by the Pimkings next week. Jessie and the babies are quite well. The newest – a model of all goodness. We spoon more with her than we have done with any of them. Best love to Oliver and kisses to the chicks, ever yr. aft. R.S.G.

Poor Mrs. Woodgate has just lost her only boy aged 3 ½ in measles. She has two girls one younger and one older than the boy.

Many thanks for the photograph of Helen Ruth. She is charmingly pretty but then so are all yr. infants.

---

*   Henry Joscelyne is recorded as having played for Upton Park Football Club in 1881/2

24/3/82

My dearest Birdie,

I have only time to add two lines to this. It seems ages since we heard of you. I hope you will not be saying the same of us. We are going on very well. All our infants flourishing. The last, Mildred May, quite the best sample of babyhood we have had. We like her better than any of them. Annie is staying with Mrs. Woodgate till Easter when she comes back to us. Trot is staying in London but I have not seen her – obliged to cut her friends the Hewetts. They are positively demoralising. Edward is becoming a more charming little companion every day. I take him on ten mile walks with me almost every Sunday. He never ceases chattering the whole time and is always most entertaining. It will be terrible to send him away to school one of these days. Best love to Alec and kisses to you and the children.

I can get you that edition of Sir W. Scott you want 48 volumes published in 1831 known as author's edition for £9.

Lakeside, Churchfield
Road, Ealing
26 January 1883

My dearest Birdie,

I have been depressed in mind since I last received a letter from you because it has been impossible for me to execute your commission to purchase a refrigerator. The fact is all the ships you mentioned by which it could come out free are at the other end of the world and the expense of carriage of an article at once so bulky and so heavy is more than I sh'd like to involve you in without more certainty. I am afraid I am not in the way of getting you a 2nd hand refrigerator. Those at the Stores are the best I could get, I suppose. I enclose the sheets of our list referring to the subject. Perhaps you will give me further instructions – and I think you could more readily ascertain at Sydney than here in London what is the cheapest method of getting it out – therefore I await your instructions on both points.

We are all very well which is the greatest point, and all very happy which is almost as great, I suppose. Our babies are making good progress. Edward can read and write a little now, and is an all round good boy, barring an occasional outburst of rebellion when we have a good deal of sound and fury signifying nothing. He has recently been executing a deliberate demonstration to assert his independence of action against Annie. It was carried out with great success during our absence for a night at Norwood. He assaulted the poor old thing and her heart nearly stopped I am afraid. However he afterwards asked her pardon in a jaunty way and obtained her forgiveness.

He went to see his first pantomime this week with Jessie – of course was immensely delighted. Most especially at the cutting up of the Clown. He remarked, however, that it was not likely that it hurt him much as he noticed that he did not bleed.

Kittens (Kitty) I think is getting pretty, or is it that one's impression of people's beauty changes with one's affection for them? At any rate for me she is more beautiful than she used to be. She is an observant little creature, e.g. on Monday last when they were playing at 'Church' and Edward was haranguing from a chair the three little ones seated on the floor, Kitty interrupted him: "Why don't you say Israel? You ought to say Israel; they always say Israel in Church!"

Effie or Josephine is the beauty of the flock and also the mistress of the nursery. She takes the lead and will not be over-ruled. The other little mite continues to give no trouble at all, enjoying the most robust health and just can walk quite alone – at 15 months old – she was born 31st October.

I was sorry to hear casually from Annie, who has been staying with Trot for a few days that Alec is laid up. I trust he is better. I see you have been having a very hot summer in Australia, which I suppose is a trial when one is seedy. We are having a very mild winter here. One day I thought that we sh'd skate the next (in December that was) but it thawed that night and we have seen neither frost nor snow since. It is a great blessing – the discomforts attending a severe winter are too great to be any compensation for the few days skating one may enjoy – and then our pipes freeze up and we can't get water either to drink or wash ourselves with. We have been without a cook for a month and Jessie has had to perform the duties of cook and maid-of-all-work during that time. We are better able to appreciate the misery you must sometimes undergo when you are cookless. Someone has said that the things that are too true pass us by as if they were not true at all, and when they have singled us out then only do they strike us – and so it is of domestic trials of this nature. Jessie is quite worn out and I am most thankful for her sake that we have got an unexceptional person coming to us next week. But the money we have paid in advertisements and in journeying about to see candidates for a situation – not to mention the loss of time and temper – all this has been pretty serious.

We have had a series of big things here (Office of Works) lately; the Review of the Egyptian troops* and the opening of

---

*   In August 1882 Sir Garnet Wolsley and an army of 20,000 invaded the Suez Canal Zone. Wolsley was authorised to crush the Urabi forces and clear the country of rebels. The decisive battle was fought at Tall al Kabir on September 13. The Urabi forces were routed and the capital captured. The nominal authority of the Khedive was restored, and the British occupation of Egypt, which was to last 72 years began.

the new Law Courts.* I had the main work of distributing the tickets and was overwhelmed with work for about a month. We were here literally till twelve o'clock at night – we are in smooth waters again now and one's prospects are I think looking up.

Trot I hear is in constant correspondence with you so I need not tell you anything of her – indeed I know very little of her proceedings and only hear of her through Percy. He and Willy often come to see us – Harry spends all his leisure at the Hewetts and there is little chance of seeing him.

Of Louisa I have had no news since I last wrote. They have a house full of pupils and should be flourishing but are not, and never will be I fear. They have not the genius. Harry Joscelyne talks of emigrating to Australia so soon as he has taken his degree at Dublin. I think he is just the man for the purpose. My best love to Oliver and to your sweet babies and kind regards to Miss Busbridge. Ever your affect. R.S.G.

I am writing at my office and am continually interrupted. Pray excuse bad writing.

The Times of 27 November 1882 wrote "As the arrangements for the state opening of the Royal Courts of Justice proceed on Monday next it becomes evident that the ceremonial is to be of unusual brilliance. The Prince and Princess of Wales and nearly all the members of the Royal Family will we understand be present. With regard to the route by which the Queen will go to the Courts from Buckingham Palace, there

---

* After a disputatious open competition, George Street had been appointed architect in 1868. He found it necessary to modify his winning design to meet the requirements of the legal profession. So significant were the alterations that in fact the final design bore little resemblance to the winning entry. Construction began in the spring of 1871 and the building was opened on 4th December 1882 by Her Majesty Queen Victoria. (Lord Chancellor's Department Press Notice 291/00 3 August 2000).

seems to be a very strong feeling that Her Majesty should be asked to pass along the more populous thoroughfare either in going or returning. Apart from the natural gratification and delight it would afford many thousands who could not safely venture in the crowds to see Her Majesty, there is the experience of the recent march of the Expeditionary Forces through the streets to speak strongly of the advantages of extending the line of principal attraction as far as possible so as to prevent an unmanageable massing of the people. Two deputations of residents in the districts principally concerned…are to wait on the Right Hon G J Shaw-Lefevre, First Commissioner of Works, today to make certain representations on the subject."

> 8, Churchfield Road,
> Ealing.W.
> 23 April 1883

My dearest Birdie,

Jessie and Annie and Mary Lake have been chattering here all together the whole even'g so that it is not till bedtime that I have been able to get peace to send you a line on your birthday – and to tell you that although we hear of each other seldom now, none the less do I wish you continually all manner of happiness – none the less do I every day regret that there is so little prospect of our ever seeing each other again. I have to congratulate you too on the birth of your fourth daughter. I have not heard from you since her birth but Trot told me of it. I hope she behaves well and does not add appreciably to your domestic labours – and that you yourself are feeling strong and well.

Our little flock here has not increased since I wrote. Our baby is just 18 months old and has never had an hour's illness – so that we have scarcely ever since we have been married been so free of anxiety about our infants. The other three are very robust and happy and are a continual delight to us. Jessie had a mild attack of measles the other day but only Kitty caught it although all 4 infants were skipping about the sick room all the time Jessie and Kitty were laid up. Percy Whitcombe, our Physician in ordinary, paid us only two visits.

You will be glad to hear he is a fine fellow. He passed his final exam M.R.C.S. on Thursday last; I think there can be no doubt he will be a great success. I did not used to think so. He seemed to lack a certain power of observation, which is most necessary to a Doctor. Practice seems to be giving him this. He is a very susceptible youth and is continually falling in love! But has a happy knack of extricating himself entirely uninjured from the most serious entanglements. Willie Whitcombe is going on remarkably well at St. Bartholomew's. He is a born Doctor. He can hardly be made to pass a lame dog in the street without stopping to diagnose his complaints and apply a remedy. He is a nice cheerful happy fellow thoroughly unselfish and kind hearted. Of Harry we have seen little of late; when he was in Town last vacation he called once to see me. He looked ill and seemed preoccupied and low-spirited. He is a very reserved youth and there was no means of learning what was on his mind.

Trot I am afraid is very hysterical about her throat. There is talk of her undergoing another operation: but Percy is against it. He is afraid of the consequences – this however you must on no account mention when writing home. What Trot needs is an entire change for a long time. I told Percy the other day that the best thing he could do with himself would be to go to Sydney, get a practice and take his mother with him. I believe if that c'd be done her life would be prolonged. Of course it is a matter for very serious consideration – and Percy himself w'd prefer remaining here I can see.

Fred Gowlland, brother of Richard Sankey

Alfred McCooper, Edward's godfather

You will be glad to hear that I have had a stroke of great good luck. The post of Ass't Secretary to our Dep't has been abolished and in its place two Principal Clerkships have been established. One of these the First Comm'r gave to me on the 1st of April. It is a splendid position and one which I could never have expected to get a few years ago. I am practically a joint Ass't Secretary to the Dept. and head of it when the Secretary is away. There are not half a dozen men of my age in the Civil Service who have attained to a post of equal importance and responsibility without political influence. My Private Secretaryship of course I have had to give up. Shaw Lefevre was very graceful in his remarks on my quitting that post and expressed much regret at losing my services which meant a good deal coming from a man the least emotional of mankind! The pay of my new appt is £1600 rising 25 per ann. to £1800 a year and as our Dept is continually increasing in importance it is not likely that we shall stop at the latter sum.

How is Oliver and why did he not write and tell me of his new daughter? I always look to getting a letter from him on these occasions at least. He has sent me 5 letters why not the 6th? Give my best love to him and kiss all the dear infants for me. Jessie sends you many tender messages. Ever your affectionate R.S.G.

Out kind regards to Miss Busbridge. I hope she is benefited by you fine climate.

8 Churchfield Road,
Ealing W
20 March 1885

My dearest Celia,

You will be sorry to hear we are in trouble. Our poor little baby was taken from us last Saturday after a week's illness. He took cold from the other children and it turned to bronchitis and then to congestion of the lungs. Jessie or I was with him continually from the beginning of his illness. He could not lie down after Monday night (He died the following Saturday) and one or other of us nursed him the whole time. He did not seem to suffer much. The difficulty in breathing seemed to exhaust him from the first, and left him in a state of stupor more or less; but he never appeared to fall asleep for more than a few minutes all the week. Jessie was much worn out and has taken the loss of the baby more to heart than even I expected. He was as you know an invalid and has scarcely been out of Jessie's sight since he was born 15 months ago. He had become a part of herself in fact, and she feels the loss even more than if he had been strong like the other children. He was buried on Tuesday at Perivale – a pretty quiet churchyard two miles from us. Jessie Edward Trot Mary Lake and myself saw him laid to rest. His little coffin was covered with white wreaths and floral crosses which kind friends had showered upon us – fitting emblems of the sweet and gentle spirit which has passed away.

Harry Whitcombe has just been here and has taken up all the time I had intended to devote to sending you a long letter. He is looking much better than when he passed through here on his way to Oxford at the beginning of the term. He is an extremely fine fellow in every respect with a disposition of the kindest and the best. He ought to make a mark in the world in whatever career he may adopt. Trot seemed extremely well and was in fine spirits. She remained with us from Monday to Wednesday and was a great comfort to Jessie. She has been spending this fortnight with Louisa who is reported to be flourishing but inconsolable at the departure of Harry and his bride. You will have met them before now I suppose. I trust Harry will soon get employment and will not regret the great step he took when he embarked for Australia. Of course when I advised him to do this I did not know that he would take a wife with him. Harry Whitcombe has quite abandoned the thought of going abroad. Percy is at his hospital still and is perfecting himself in the healing art. I consider he is an excellent doctor with a real taste for his profession.

All my infants are well. For Edward, I have just had an invitation to spend a month at Westgate at Easter with my Secretary's family – Mr Mitford. His boy was born the same day as Edward. He and the Lady Clementine Mitford take an interest in Edward.

I must now say goodbye. With my best love to Oliver and kisses to all your babies. Believe me always y'r aff'ate R.S.G.

I am writing at my office in the midst of perpetual interruptions. I hope you will like H. Joscelyne. He is a very genuine persevering straightforward fellow. We are all greatly rejoiced and pleased at the help coming from NSW for our campaign in Egypt[*]. It is the most significant fact and the only comforting one in all the miserable

business. Has Oliver read Seeley's Expansion of England? He sh'd do so.

---

[*]   The revolt of the Mahdi in the Sudan. General Gordon was sent to evacuate the territory, was besieged in Khartoum by the Mahdi and killed. The troops from New South Wales arrived too late.

8 Churchfield Road,
Ealing.
7 September 1885

My dearest Celia,

I am continually ashamed of myself for letting so long a time elapse without writing to you. But in fact I write to no one now. I am growing increasingly idle and find I can always quiet my conscience by the reflection that I really have not a word to say or a sentiment to express which it is worthwhile to write upon paper. This is what the Germans call "Grobian"* though; and is a state of mind which sh'd be sat upon, and I really do mean to write to you more often in the future. I haven't even heard of you since your and Oliver's letters reached me in which you spoke of our poor little lost baby. Since then we have had another little son added to our flock. He is a perfect beauty and we have never felt so proud of any of our infants before. Jessie looks five years younger only from laughing at him and he is altogether the greatest joy of the house. If we were not in a chronic state of impecuniosity we should get his photograph taken in order that you might rejoice over his big blue eyes and frank open face and broad shoulders and fat legs! The other infants are and have been well. Mildred Mary, known to us by her own rendering of that name as Doody Dary, the next youngest is 3 and very delightful in her baby prattle. None of our former children have talked such beautiful baby talk. She has the happiest way of twisting hard words into the compass of her own powers of pronunciation. And her words are so pretty while she ?twists that I am afraid that the whole household adopts her rendering in preference to the vernacular; and if you could drop out of the sky to listen to our talk in the nursery you would think we were

*	loutish or clownish.

all as mad as march hares! I consider she is growing a very nice looking child in spite of her early promise to be an ugly duckling. The next eldest is Josephine Miriam "Effie" and she and Kitty are both now losing their baby plumpness and roundness and are thinner and paler. Kitty is the angel of the house who composes differences and "gives up". Effie asserts her rights through thick and thin and is always prepared to claw anyone who attempts to defraud her of them. She is therefore at the present moment the chief concern of the nursery and spends much of her time "in Coventry". Edward's character is much the same as hers. He is also very pale and thin and his delicate appearance excites much sympathy. He is in fact always well and contrives to get through an immense quantity of physical exercise without breaking down. He will be nine when you get this – or soon after – 14 December. I am not satisfied with his school and shall send him elsewhere after Xmas. I am anxious that he should be worked up to go to St Paul's School when he is 12. He would go as a day boy by train every day. I sh'd prefer sending him away but I see no prospect of being able to afford it. He went with me to spend 10 days with Cooper at Brighton last month. We bathed in the sea 8 days out of the ten and I contrived to teach him to swim that is to say he was able to swim out of his depth and keep afloat a reasonable time but I don't say that I w'd like to see him pitched into deep water just yet. But he would swim perfectly well now in a week. It was very amusing to see his little head rising above the waves when he was out of his depth puffing and blowing and struggling in the water like a young puppy. He has been often on the river with me this summer and rows now fairly well. We often make expeditions to the Thames touching the river at various places where the Great Western has stations and coming back in the evening. This year owing to the change of Government and the illness of my Secretary I have been able to take only 18 instead of 40 days leave and feel entitled to consider myself a martyr in consequence. I am however so remarkably well that I do not much lament the missing days. I have played tennis every day so long as the light lasted since the early part of May and the exercise has done me no end of good and although I am getting to look desperately old I am feeling younger and stronger than I ever did in my whole life. Indeed it is for me quite an effort to realise that I am upon the verge of 40. I seem to have no sympathy with the men of 40 and find myself at tennis and elsewhere invariably consorting with young men who when they see my bald head and almost white hair must think they are cracking jokes with a grandfather. Jessie is always reproving me for my childish antics. She is solemnity itself compared to me! I am most thankful to say that she also was never better and has moreover taken to have an appetite which is quite a novelty in our married experience. I am sorry that she has not been away for a change this year and last, but she has preferred to stay at home with the baby and we both very much doubt the wisdom of taking children into seaside lodgings. Some friends of ours at Ealing hired a house at the sea and immediately afterwards – only the other day – found they had scarlet fever! We are building ambitious castles in the air – and yet we hope not in the air – for next year. We intend if it is in any way possible to have one month of unrivalled splendour in Switzerland and thereafter to roll up our tents and give up any further attempt at seeing the world. I wish with all my heart you were coming with us. I have written a most egotistical gossip, but at any rate it is about the subject I understand! Do please send me three sheets back about your husband and babies! Give them my best love and with kisses to yourself believe me your most affectionate R.S.G.

My love to Harry Joscelyne and my respects to his wife. How are they getting on? Not one word have I heard about them since they left. I have had one letter from Louisa all that time and that epistle was so freezingly cold that I have had no desire to continue the correspondence.

CPI Antony Rowe

Chippenham, UK

2018-08-03 15:40